A SURPRISING DIVERSION

When Galen grinned, Phoebe was shocked more than she had been at anything tonight. "This should be fun."

"Fun?"

"Yes. Although the Season is just underway, it seems to be picking up exactly where the last Little Season ended. Mayhap I have come to London for too many Seasons, because all I can see ahead of me here is ennui and playing chaperon for my brother. Helping you should be much more fun."

She stared at him. This was not a game. This was life and death, the lives of those she helped and her death if she were caught. He had to understand that.

"Galen, if you were to be connected with me, you could be ruined or sent to hang with me."

He waved her words aside. "Your warning may be too late, Phoebe. It should not take long for them to connect the lady in my carriage with you. All they need do is look at a portrait of you in your house, and they will know that the beautiful woman in my arms was you. Blast! I should have hidden your hair. I don't want us stopped before we leave London. . . ."

Phoebe stared at him as he spoke. One minute, Galen treated this like a game arranged for his private amusement. The next, he was as serious as a judge pronouncing sentence. Yet, even if he were mad, he was the only ally she had now. . . .

Also by Jo Ann Ferguson

HIS LADY
MIDNIGHT

Jo Ann Ferguson

ZEBRA BOOKS
Kensington Publishing Corp.
http://www.zebrabooks.com

ZEBRA BOOKS are published by

Kensington Publishing Corp.
850 Third Avenue
New York, NY 10022

All Kensington titles, imprints, and distributed lines are
available at special quantity discounts for bulk purchases for
sales promotions, premiums, fund-raising, educational or in-
stitutional use.

Special book excerpts or customized printings can also be
created to fit specific needs. For details, write or phone the
office of the Kensington Special Sales Manager: Kensington
Publishing Corp., 850 Third Avenue, New York, NY 10022.
Attn. Special Sales Department. Phone: 1-800-221-2647.

Zebra and the Z logo Reg. U.S. Pat. & TM Off.

First Printing: September 2001
10 9 8 7 6 5 4 3 2 1

Printed in the United States of America

For Bruce Todd
For more reasons than I could ever list

One

It was a night perfect for subterfuge. The moon was lost behind clouds, and the wind-driven rain blurred the few lights along the docks. By the wharves, the ships strained and creaked, eager to be on their way along the Thames and out to sea. Distant church bells sounded the hour as the poor huddling in the city's hovels tried to sleep while the *ton* gossiped and frolicked with flirtations through yet another early spring night.

The only thing missing, Lady Phoebe Brackenton decided, was one of London's notorious smoke-filled fogs. That was all to the good because the fog was seldom her ally on these nights when she was found where no one would guess she might be. Frightened people who were being given a second chance at the life they thought was forever lost could slip and hurt themselves on a mist-dampened wharf. They could become lost all too easily, she had learned, risking their lives and hers. And those who sought to halt her could sneak up on her before she even knew they were nearby.

A shadow crossed in front of her carriage. She no longer flinched each time someone came close. In the five years since she had embarked on what others would call madness and what she considered her obligation, she had learned that panic was her worst enemy. It threatened her more than the severe laws of England, which sent petty criminals, many who broke the law simply to provide food and shelter for their families, to the far side of the world to Botany Bay and the other penal colonies. Fear could betray her to the very judges who had no compassion for people who would be separated from their families for the rest of their lives, because few would be able to afford the passage home to England at the end of their sentence.

"All is ready, m'lady," came the voice she had been waiting to hear.

She nodded, not correcting Jasper who knew better than to use her title here on the wharves. Again she ignored the fright taunting her. Even if a Charley chanced to hear, most of the night watchmen along the docks could be bribed if they were sober enough to take heed of her and her allies.

"How many tonight?" she asked as she pulled her ebony cloak more tightly around her. The Season had only begun, so the chill of winter still clung to the night here by the water.

" 'E was able to get an even dozen out 'fore the cap'n took count of 'eads." Jasper's pride swelled through his voice.

She smiled. Twelve was a lucky number. They could easily fit twelve people in the closed wagon waiting behind a stack of barrels only a few paces along the wharf. Finding a place for them to hide later might be a problem, but she had faced worse challenges since she had embarked on this dual life. It had begun the day she had learned about the fearsome fate of a young man from the church whose living belonged to her family. He had been caught poaching on a neighboring estate and had been sentenced to seven years' transportation to the Australian penal colonies. She had found a way to smuggle him off the ship bound for Australia and then obtained him a job far from the shire. There he would stay in exile for the seven years of his sentence, but he could return to his family at the end of the time.

"Thank you, Jasper," she said, dropping two packets into his hand. One was for the ship's crewman who had risked his life to help. The other was Jasper's. He would arrange for the escaped convicts to be taken to sheep farms in Exmoor that were always looking for workers and never asked any questions. "Can you be back here in a fortnight? The *Trellis* is supposed to be sailing by then."

"I shall be 'ere, m'lady." He clamped his hand over his mouth and rushed away.

Phoebe hit the side of the carriage with the flat of her hand. It turned away from the river and rushed back toward Mayfair. Her coachee, Sam, had taken to this type of ruse with the same skill he brought to driving. If she had not had these excellent allies and her determination to help these people, she might have surrendered to her panic long ago.

She clasped her fingers, which were atremble. Whispering a prayer that, once again, they would escape detection, she took a deep breath, then another to slow her rapid heartbeat. To own the truth, she wished she could say tonight's excursion had been her last, but she knew that was not so. Until the laws of England were changed so the sentence reflected the breadth of the crime, she could not halt helping those who needed her.

Lights glittered into the carriage, and Phoebe smiled. They had returned to Mayfair where the dark was unwelcome. The countess's house was as bright as if a thousand stars had settled within its windows.

A single footman stood on the walkway, for the guests had all arrived hours ago. Lady Beterley's soirees were as de rigueur as a night at Almack's for those who wished to be counted among the elite of the elite.

Shrugging off her ebony cloak, Phoebe smiled when the footman opened the carriage door. She accepted his hand as he helped her to the walkway and nodded when he asked her if the fresh air had helped settle her stomach. With a smile, she reminded herself that she had not lied to the kind man. Her stomach had been roiling like a pot of soup in the hour before she slipped out of the party. Serenity, in her case, was only skin deep.

As she entered the foyer that was eye-wrenchingly bright with its dozens of candles reflecting off gilt and painted friezes, Phoebe glanced toward the glass hanging at the foot of the stairs leading up to where voices and music flowed together. Except for wilted feathers on the *eau de Nile* turban that matched her gown with its fashionably high bodice and ruffles at the hem of both her sleeves and her skirt, she looked no different than when she had left this gathering. A ride about Hanover Square to take the air would have left the feathers drooping too, so nothing about her should betray where she had been.

She turned to rush up the stairs and collided with something as unyielding as the side of a ship. When she rocked back, broad hands caught her shoulders to steady her.

"I am so sorry, sir," she said. "I failed to look where I was going, and . . ." Even knowing she was showing a want for sense, she could not halt herself. She stared up at the man in front of her.

The man was uncommonly handsome and uncommonly well known throughout the Polite World. With hair as dark as the cloak she had left in the carriage and eyes only a shade lighter, Galen Townsend, third viscount, had a reputation for appreciating the company of the ladies and the camaraderie of his tie-mates at his club in St. James's. She had heard whispers of how his firmly sculpted face could change from one expression to the next in the midst of a heartbeat, a heartbeat that was sure to gather speed if it were within a woman's breast. Other rumors had not been so complimentary, but she did not believe all that was *on dits*. After all, rumors had often suggested she was about to accept a proposal. One rumor was about a man she had never even met who was reported to have offered for her.

"Steady there, my lady." Lord Townsend's smile was as scintillating as she had heard. His eyes were warm, not like the cold stare that was whispered about whenever he was not near. "Excuse me for being in such a hurry that I nearly knocked you from your feet."

"I should have watched where I was going."

"You should leave that task to the gentlemen who would delight in watching where you go." He dipped his head toward her. "Galen, Lord Townsend, my lady."

"And I am—"

"Phoebe Brackenton, if I am not mistaken," he said with another smile.

"You are not."

"I am glad, because I would be quite the rogue not to recall the name of the prettiest lady at this assembly, would I not?"

She wished she had a fan, for the foyer was suddenly a bit too warm. It must be because she had been out in the night for so long. Jasper had despaired of the crew ever getting anyone off the ship tonight, and she had wondered if she would take a chill in the gown that was meant for a more seasonable Season instead of the damp cool by the river.

"You are too kind, my lord." She stepped back, realizing belatedly how close they stood. "And I am being most impolite to keep you from your destination."

"My destination?"

His puzzlement had a boyish charm that tempted her to smile in return. Mayhap she would have, if she had given his expression any credence. Lord Townsend had been the subject of too many whispered asides for her to believe he was doing anything but hoaxing her.

"You appeared to be in a hurry, my lord."

"Did I? I thought you did not see me." He rested one arm on the banister and grinned. "To go unnoticed until one is run into is quite a blow to one's vanity, especially when I am attired in dandy-set style."

Phoebe was certain he was jesting with her now, because his coat was a sedate navy and his waistcoat and breeches a proper white. Although his cravat was tied with a fashionable flourish, his collar did not reach to his ears in the style the foppish among the *ton* would have chosen.

"Forgive me if I have given you insult, my lord. I should have blamed my own absentmindedness."

"Or mayhap it was the fact that you were trying to sneak back in here like a child who has tripped his governess the double."

She pressed her hand to her bodice. Now her heart *was*, as other women had reported after being in Lord Townsend's company, beating like the hooves of a runaway horse. How had the viscount guessed the truth? No, she must not give into panic. He could not know the truth. He simply must have seen her coming through the door. Warning herself to remain calm before she betrayed herself and all those who depended on her, she forced a smile.

"Do not, I implore you," she said quietly, "tell our hostess that I found the odor of the men's cigars a bit overwhelming even in the ballroom, so I went out to seek some fresher air."

"Such words will remain locked in my heart forever." He put his hand over the center of his waistcoat, and she could not help noting the breadth of his chest. When he took her hand, her fingers were dwarfed by his. She sensed the strength in those fingers, but they were gentle as he bowed over them. "I would not think of bringing distress to our hostess or more to you, my lady."

"Thank you." Why were words so impossible to find now? Usually she could talk about anything to anyone, but trite words were the best she could do when his earth brown eyes gazed down at her, sparkling as if they were decorated with a heated mist.

"My pleasure, my lady." He bowed over her hand again.

When a beguiling warmth grazed her skin through her kid gloves, she clenched her other hand by her side. The mere brush of his breath should not have such an unsettling effect on her. Galen Townsend was a prime rake who dabbled in flirtations without thought of the consequences of the broken hearts left in his wake. She knew better than this. She was no lass right out of the schoolroom, who dreamed of a lord sweeping her off her feet with promises of love and marriage. No, her life was different, for it had obligations she could share with no one but her few allies in the night. Certainly, her life had no place for a dalliance with a dashing blade.

Mayhap if Parliament would change the country's appalling laws, she could think of . . . Was she want-witted? This was Galen Townsend who was filling her head with fantasies as he had too many women before her. They had come to grief, but she would not be the same.

Drawing her fingers out of his, she whispered, "Good evening, Lord Townsend." She rushed up the stairs before that enticing smile could convince her to be the next air-dreamer to be bamblusterated by his undeniable charm.

Why did the *ton* have to rush back to London before spring arrived? This winter had been colder than most, and it was proving reluctant to let spring return.

As he waited for his carriage to be brought, Galen Townsend glanced back at the countess's house. Lady Phoebe must have been quite overmastered by the smoke, because he had been sure that she had been gone for more than an hour. He probably would not have noticed that fact, except that he had seen her talking to Carr before his brother vanished. Had he and Lady Phoebe gone for a ride without the eyes of a watchdog?

Impossible. Even if Lady Phoebe's reputation was not as pristine as the pearls that emphasized her slender throat, his brother preferred brunettes. Carr might have made an exception for Lady Phoebe, Galen thought with a taut smile, because her hair, blond though it might be, had a lustrous glow that intrigued a man, urging him to touch it to discover if the strands were sunshine warm. With eyes as blue as a sunlit summer sky, she had drawn his own eyes over and over before she took her leave at about the same time Carr had.

Why hadn't he asked her if she had been with his brother? Again impossible. Such a question could have gained him a slap across his face, and it would have been justified. He could not tarnish a lady's reputation simply because he was worried about what his brother would do next to blemish their family's already besmirched honor.

The carriage rattled to a stop in front of him. Looking up, he said to his coachman, "Let's start with the usual places, Alfred."

"As you wish, my lord."

Galen did not reply as he climbed into the elegant carriage and settled back against the leather seats that had been recently cleaned. The odor of the soap assailed him, and he fought not to sneeze.

How many more nights was he going to ride through the streets of London trying to halt his brother from drowning in his own folly? He knew the answer. He would do it as long as he must, although he would have liked to remain at the countess's soirée tonight and probe further to discover what Lady Phoebe Brackenton had truly been doing. Mayhap the smoke had disturbed her, but he suspected she had been less than honest with him about what she had been doing during her time away from the gathering.

He heard his name shouted. Even though he did not want to halt now, he slapped his hand against the side of the carriage, stopping it before it had traveled far from the square. He opened the door as a rider paused next to it.

"Galen, I had hoped to speak with you before you departed tonight." Sir Ledwin Woods swung down from his horse. He was a plump man with a heart as big as his stomach, and he had been Galen's friend since they first attended school together as boys. Galen was not surprised that Ledwin was only now on his way to the countess's party, because Ledwin often lost himself in his reading for days at a time, only realizing belatedly that he had missed some appointment he had made and had intended to keep . . . this time. His work had increased since he had been given some minor post in the government. Galen was not even sure what it might be.

As Ledwin came over to the carriage, he said, "I trust from your exasperated expression that you are again on your way to save Carr from his own imprudence."

"He has been gone for too long, I fear." He sighed as he climbed out and clasped his friend's outstretched hand. "And you know how much trouble he can find with such little effort."

"I thought he was still abed with that fever he caught earlier in the month."

Galen flinched.

"Forgive me," Ledwin hurried to say, putting his hand on Galen's shoulder in sympathy. "I should not have reminded you of that."

"You did not remind me. The truth is that I cannot forget." He clasped his hands behind his back, his fingers curling into fists. "If he had died from that fever, his death would have been my fault."

Ledwin scowled, the furrows in his forehead looking even deeper in the faint light from the carriage's lantern. "You have taken on the task of being your brother's keeper when he does not want you to help him. That is a thankless task, Galen, which may gain you only more trouble."

"No matter. The task is mine."

"You will never change him from seeking his entertainments in ignoble taphouses as long as you remain in London."

"The Season—"

"Will go on without the Townsend brothers." He chuckled. "Do you worry about Carr missing his entertainments, Galen, or you missing yours? I hear that, although the Season is but a week old, already two lasses are vowing never to marry unless they can claim the title of Lady Townsend."

"You should not heed poker-talk." He put his hand back on the door. "I cannot linger. I must find Carr and get him back home."

"Berkeley Square is too close to Drury Lane and the other places where he can seek trouble."

"What would you suggest? That I purchase one of the new homes they are building in Regent's Park?"

Ledwin sighed. "Too close still, I fear. Why don't you persuade Carr to spend some time at Thistlewood Cottage?"

"Your country seat in Bath?" Galen laughed and shook his head. "I appreciate your generosity, my friend, but Carr will no more leave London during the Season than—"

"You would?"

Again Galen flinched. To own the truth, he enjoyed the Season with its gatherings and its gossip and its flirtations. If Carr enjoyed only that, Galen would have had no worries.

His brother had sought baser entertainments during the past year, leading him more deeply into trouble that tempted him to more. At first, Galen had thought Carr would come to realize he was choosing the wrong sports, but Carr reveled in them, pursuing them night after night and not returning until long past dawn.

That was why, when Carr did not come home two weeks ago when the night was exceptionally cold, Galen had not worried. Then, in the morning, a footman had found Carr half dead with the cold on the front steps. Carr had been so altogethery that he had not realized that he was only inches from his own door.

When the fever struck, nearly killing Carr, Galen had hoped it would persuade his brother to rethink his life. Mayhap it had, because now Carr seemed even more determined to waste his life in high, fast living in low taverns.

"Excuse me, Ledwin," he said as he stepped back into his carriage. "I must be on my way in hopes of finding Carr in one of his usual places."

"They grow in number."

"Yes."

"As does your burden, my friend."

"It is *my* burden, and I must tend to it."

Ledwin nodded and closed the carriage door. Folding his arms on the window, he said, "My offer stands for whenever you have need of Thistlewood Cottage. Consider it."

"I shall."

"I hope you find him quickly."

Galen slapped the side of the carriage as his friend stepped aside. "So do I," he said under his breath. "So do I."

Two

It was taking too long. They had to get this night's work done and be on their way before anyone took note of what they were doing.

Phoebe heard shouts and pushed open the door of her carriage. She waved aside her coachman, but Sam clung close to her as she edged toward the wagon that should have been on its way before now. What was causing the delay?

"Go back to the carriage, Sam," she ordered as she peered around a stack of what might have been raw cotton or finished textiles.

"My lady, I should stay with you."

She shook her head. "I need you ready with the carriage, so we can leave posthaste if we must."

"I don't like any of this."

Neither did she. Tonight was one of those fogbound nights when disaster lurked unseen. The sudden turn of the weather from winter to spring brought these fogs, which were at their worst here by the Thames. Hearing the muffled clang of church bells in the distance, she gasped. An hour had passed since she had arrived, and still the task for tonight was not completed.

She glanced over her shoulder and saw Sam remained close behind her. "Go!"

"My lady—"

"Say nothing!" She put her hand on his arm to soften the impact of her sharp words.

When he nodded and turned reluctantly to follow her orders, she promised herself that she would apologize to him once they were back on Grosvenor Square. Another shudder raced through her as she thought of her beloved home, which was now mortgaged for more than it was worth. Helping others had come at a high price, and she was unsure how much longer she could live among the *ton* and still do this work. Greater bribes were being demanded with every ship that was readied to sail from the Pool to Australia. Her family's estate in Kent must sell soon, or she would lose both it and her house here in Town.

You could stop this.

She ignored the tempting voice as she had since she had embarked on this crusade. Yes, she could halt this, but then the innocents among the true criminals would be punished for a crime no greater than stealing five shillings' worth of bread from a shop or setting a trap to catch a rabbit on some unfeeling peer's land.

Seeing a familiar form through the contortions of the fog, Phoebe inched around the stack of bales. A mistake, she discovered, as Jasper turned and, in a hint of breeze that swept aside the fog, she saw another man beyond him. It was too late. She could not turn back now, because she had been seen.

She pulled the hood of her cloak over her bonnet to hide its quality. She kept her arms close to her, so no one would see the silver bracelet around her left wrist. Bother! She would have left it on Grosvenor Square if she had had any idea that she must step into the discussions on the wharf. Letting the cloak's hem drag in the puddles on the wharf so that she looked as bedraggled as Jasper, she hoped the man was from the *Trellis*.

"What're ye doin' 'ere?" Jasper muttered, stepping between her and the other man who was watching her closely through narrowed eyes.

"Seein' what's keepin' ye." She tried to make her accent as broad as his, but she glanced at the other man. For someone who spent so much time near water, she doubted if he had used any to bathe in weeks. His clothes reeked so much that her eyes watered. His matted hair was as dark as Lord Townsend's.

Why was she thinking of *him* now? She must concentrate on this bumble-bath and find a way to complete the night's work without compromising Jasper or herself. Biting back the questions she longed to ask, she knew she had to wait for Jasper to tell her what was wrong and how she could help. Her fan and reticule bounced against her leg as she moved closer to Jasper, and she hoped her heavy cloak would hide the motions from this sailor. She did not want him to think about the possibility that her bag contained gold. She wanted him to keep his mind firmly on completing the deal that would allow them to get the innocents off the boat.

"Woman, ye aren't needed 'ere," Jasper answered. "This be men's business."

She slid her arm through his as she noted two other shadowed forms behind the sailor. Mayhap she should have heeded Sam's concern and let him come with her. He was a big man and strong, and he would have forced anyone who might be thinking of doing something foolish to think again. A single shout would bring him running, but she did not want to tip her hand until absolutely necessary.

"Ye've been gone so long," she said. "I got tired of waitin' on ye."

"We ain't got time for no curtain lecture from yer woman," growled the sailor. "Told ye what we want."

"And I told ye it was too much. I already offered ye two guineas more than last time. It'll be the best I can do."

"Not enough for my mates and me." He squinted. " 'Ow 'bout the lass? She got some gold on 'er?"

"The missus ain't got nothin' worth nothin'." Jasper edged Phoebe a half step behind him as he added, "Told ye my best offer."

"Ain't good enough."

"Then we've got nothin' more to say to ye. If ye don't want my price, then I shall find someone who will."

"Jasper!" she whispered. "We can't go without—"

He scowled at her. "This ain't yer business, woman."

As he turned her to walk away, the sailor shouted, "Wait!"

"Ain't got nothin' left to say." Jasper kept walking.

"Wait!" called the man.

"Jasper," she whispered, "if they want to negotiate, we have to listen to them."

"Give it a minute. They'll be beggin' us to come back." He chuckled softly. "Some of the tars are just more stubborn than the others. In a minute, they'll—"

Something exploded through the night. Phoebe gasped as Jasper reeled against her, knocking her into some barrels. When he cursed, she pulled him away from the stack as it began to wobble. The barrels toppled to the wharf with a crash that was not as ear shattering as the first explosion.

Jasper began to run through the swirls of the fog, tugging her after him. She did not hesitate. Gathering up her skirt, she followed. Then she passed him. In amazement, she turned. She had never been able to outrun Jasper, even though she was two years older than him and had been trying to best him since they were children on her father's estate in Kent.

"Jasper, what's wrong?"

"They got me." All hints of his dockside accent vanished, warning her that something was terribly amiss.

"Got you?"

He pulled her behind a stack of wooden cases and down an alley. When he reached a corner, he peered along it. She had no idea what he hoped to see as the fog grew even thicker. He drew her to the left. He threw open a door, then closed it behind them.

Phoebe paid no attention to the scent of horses that warned they were in the back of a stable. When Jasper collapsed to the ground, his hand pressed to his right thigh, she knelt beside him. She pushed aside his hand, even though he warned her away.

Blood glistened in the dim light. Slipping her hand under his leg, she smiled grimly as her bracelet jangled against the stone floor. Damp there, too. That was good, because the ball must have gone clear through the flesh of his leg. Reaching into her bodice, she pulled out a kerchief and pressed it to the wound.

He groaned, but ordered, "Go! You can't be seen here."

"But you—"

She was amazed when he grinned. "I've come to know these docks better than the river rats do. They have not caught me before this. They won't catch me tonight."

"I can't leave you hurt."

"I shall be fine. The chap who takes care of the beasts here is a friend." He muttered something under his breath, something she was sure she should not ask him to repeat more loudly. "If you go right out to the front, the carriage should be just to your left."

"So close?"

"Aye. Arranged that with Sam." He shoved her hand off his leg and put his own over the cloth. "Go, so I can get out of here myself. I don't want those chaps to take aim on me again."

Phoebe stood. "Why did they shoot at us?"

"Do you want my guess?"

"Yes."

"Could be they were not sea-crabs at all."

"Not sailors?" She stared at him, not wanting to believe his words or that he had been shot.

"Get out of here, m'lady, before they take it in their minds to give chase." Pushing himself to his feet, he pulled a strip off the bottom of his shirt. He wrapped it around his leg. "They didn't get a good look at you, and—"

"Someone's back 'ere!" The bellow rang through the low ceiling of the stable.

Jasper pulled her out through the door and shoved her in one direction along the alley as he ran in the other, vanishing within a pair of steps into the fog. Phoebe wanted to call after him, but another shout from the stable sent her racing into the labyrinth of the riverside alleys.

Tonight had gone all wrong from the onset. First, she had not been able to find a way to sneak away from the duke's musicale. Everyone in attendance seemed determined to speak with her and ask her opinion of the evening's entertainment. That problem seemed like only an irritation now as she hurried through the foul passages between the houses. Shouts followed her, spurring her feet until a twinge in her side became a knot of pain.

She leaned back in the shadows and tried to listen for sounds of pursuit. Nothing, but she knew the fog could deaden noise and make it sound as if it were coming from a completely different direction. Holding her breath, she listened again. She heard shouts from within a house and the clatter of horseshoes on broken cobbles. Straining, she sought the hushed whisper of the river edging past the wharves. She needed to go in that direction, and she was not sure where exactly the river was. None of these alleys were straight.

As she pushed herself away from the filthy wall, she glanced back the way she had come. *Stay safe, Jasper.* It was a simple prayer, but it was the best she could do when she was so scared and her sides ached.

Quickly Phoebe discovered she was utterly lost. All hopes of finding her carriage were dashed when she emerged onto a street that was lit by a single lamp. A stench, almost as foul as the odor of the unwashed sailor, filled every breath. She peered at a sign hanging in front of a tavern, The Little Lost Lamb. She had never seen this place before. Looking both ways, she tried to decide which direction led to the river and which to Mayfair.

Had they been betrayed? Was that what Jasper had been about to say when they were forced to flee?

She trembled at the very thought. For five years, there had been rumors of her work. She had heard them herself among the *ton,* but she had acted no more interested in them than in the Prince Regent's latest peccadillo. She had hoped that would put an end to the speculation that the laws of England that transported people for inconsequential offenses to Botany Bay were being circumvented with the help of a member of the *ton* who could afford to pay bribes to buy silence.

Someone must have decided to offer even more

gold to loosen a few tongues. She must think about what she would do next, but first she had to get back to Grosvenor Square and send someone to find out if Jasper was all right. Of one thing she was certain. He would never betray her to the authorities, for it had been his younger brother she had first saved from being transported.

Phoebe stared as she turned a corner, then smiled as she saw a bulky shape appear out of the wafting fog. A carriage! Was it hers? No, its wheels were painted a bright green that even the dim light could not disguise. It was a gentleman's carriage, built for speed. And it was just what she needed.

Not pausing to ease her curiosity about why a gentleman would be in this disgusting place at this hour, she kept to the shadows. She did not want the coachman to see her. The thought of leaving a gentleman here while she borrowed his carriage to get back to Grosvenor Square bothered her, but she would find a way to apologize. No doubt, the gentleman would be so glad to avoid speaking of being down here by the Thames that he would forgive her if she said nothing of where she had found the carriage.

When she was sure the coachman could not see her, she threw open the door and climbed in. Hitting the side of the carriage with the flat of her hand, she gripped the window as the coachman whipped up the horses. She had no idea where they might be heading, but, for the moment, that did not matter. All she cared about was betwattling her pursuers and returning to the duke's musicale before anyone noticed she was no longer among the guests.

Closing her eyes, she leaned back against the seat. *Stay safe, Jasper.* The plea repeated itself over and over through her head. He had risked his life to protect her, and she hoped that, even now, he had found his way to her carriage and Sam was taking him to Grosvenor Square where Jasper's wound could be tended. Mayhap she should go there herself. No, she needed to return to the duke's gathering so, if questions arose, she could honestly say she had been in attendance for most of the night.

"Would you be so kind as to tell me where we are bound?"

As the voice emerged from the other side of the carriage, Phoebe grasped the edge of the seat. She turned and stared at the shadows, which moved and became a man's silhouette that was as dark and mysterious as his voice.

A voice that was familiar, but whose was it? She hoped it was someone she could trust. Yet whom could she trust now? The authorities might be seeking her, if those sailors had been sent there by the government to trap her. She could not jump to conclusions. Too much was unknown. She must not panic. She must not.

"Do you have no answer for me, my lady?"

Although she still could not guess who might be sitting beside her, his features lost in the night, she said, "Forgive me. I had no idea anyone else—that is—"

"I understand, Lady Phoebe."

"Do you?" She wondered how she had betrayed her identity when she could not guess his. Then she guessed he had seen her illuminated by some faint light when she entered the carriage. Next time, she must be more careful. Oh, she hoped there would never be another set of disasters like this night's.

"Of course." He leaned toward her, and his face was lit by a streetlamp they passed.

Phoebe wanted to groan with despair. Lord Townsend! She should have guessed only a man of his ill repute would leave his carriage sitting in plain view on such a despicable street. Had he been waiting for someone? Heat climbed her face as she wondered if she had intruded on an assignation. She shook aside the thought. Galen Townsend's reputation was not pristine, but she had never heard his name connected with a Cyprian. That, in retrospect, was odd, but she had no time to consider that now.

When she did not answer, he went on, "Of course, I understand. You did not expect anyone to be a witness to your crime."

"My crime?" The skills that had become instinct over the past five years kept her voice even and her hands from shaking. She had no idea how much he could discern in the darkness. She wished she could see more, so she might gauge his expression and decide how best to extract herself from this predicament.

"Of trying to abscond with my carriage."

"Oh, that crime."

Her relieved reply was a mistake, she realized, when he asked, "What other crime did you think I meant?"

Tonight she was prepared. She flipped open her fan and wafted it in front of her face, just in case he still could see more than she in the poor light. "Lord Townsend, do not hoax me now. I have had an evening I wish never to repeat."

"Is that so?"

"Yes, I believe I just said so."

"And your word is always the truth?"

"I try always to be honest. Lying is not a habit one should embark on carelessly."

"You are correct. One lie often leads to another."

She took a deep breath and released it slowly. She must keep her voice even. "I agree."

"I'm glad that we are in agreement on the most basic of matters. And I'm sure you'll agree as well that it's time we should spread a bit of light over this murky situation. I know I would appreciate being enlightened about several matters I find baffling."

Phoebe blinked as Lord Townsend lit the lamp near the roof. Raising her hands to block the sudden burst of light, she wished he had warned her so she might have covered her eyes. Since she had left the duke's townhouse, her eyes had become accustomed to the foggy night.

"What the . . . ?" He grasped her hands.

"My lord, what are you doing?"

Instead of answering, he tilted her hands toward him. She gasped as she looked down at them. Dried blood filled every crease of her palms.

Raising his gaze to hers, he said, "I think, my lady, it is time you told me all of the truth."

Three

Galen had never seen a face as colorless as Lady Phoebe Brackenton's as she stared at the telltale stains on her hands. He could not begin to imagine why a lady, who should not be beyond the boundaries of the Polite World in Mayfair or Bloomsbury, had rushed into his carriage here by the Pool. And with blood on her hands like Lady Macbeth.

Not just on her hands, for a scarlet patch was drying to a dull brown on the front of her skirt. He frowned. Her cloak must have fallen open so that her gown had come in contact with the blood. But whose blood was it?

His first pinch of horror that the blood belonged to the lady herself had been wrong. She was unharmed. Frightened, yes, but that was understandable in light of the blood splattered on her. Now he wanted an explanation of why she had almost thrown herself into his carriage, interrupting yet another search for his wayward brother. His first inclination to turn the carriage about and continue looking for Carr had dissolved when he had seen Lady Phoebe's terror. She needed him more than his brother did, and being needed instead of being considered a pest was a pleasant change. The circumstances for Lady Phoebe were apparently not at all pleasant.

"My lady?"

She did not answer him even though he pushed aside his cape to put his hand on her shoulder.

"My lady?"

She continued to stare at her hands as if she had never seen them before.

"Lady Phoebe?" He put one finger beneath her chin and tipped it back, bringing her eyes up toward his.

She blinked, but did not speak.

"Phoebe?" he asked softly. "Tell me what happened to you."

"I must not." She tried to turn away, but he cupped her chin, keeping her looking at him. "Please, my lord. If you would take me to my house on Grosvenor Square, I would be grateful."

"And you would be grateful if I were to say nothing of this."

Her eyes brightened. "Would you?"

"That depends."

"On what?"

"On you telling me the truth of what happened to you." When she started to protest, he put his finger to her lips. Her breath burst out in a gasp of amazement at his brazen action, and he let its softness sift along his skin before he added, "I was waiting for my brother when you commandeered this carriage. I need to know if he is in any danger."

"I don't know anything about your brother's whereabouts."

"How do I know if that is the truth?"

"I told you that I always try to be truthful."

"Then I believe you need to try harder."

"I have told you all I can."

"Forgive me, Phoebe, but I don't believe that." He

reached up for the hatch in the roof. Throwing it open, he called to his coachee, "Take us back to the Little Lost Lamb, Alfred. I—"

"No!" she cried, grabbing his arm. "Don't take me back there. I beg you."

He stared at her fear. It could not have been feigned, but he guessed her tranquility had been. She was afraid of what might be waiting for her back there. As he lifted her bloodstained hand off his sleeve, he guessed she had cause to be.

"Very well," he said, resisting the yearning to relent when her wide eyes glittered with unshed tears. He raised his voice. "Take us home to Berkeley Square, Alfred." He closed the hatch.

"But my home is on the east side of Grosvenor Square," Phoebe whispered.

"I realize that. I realize as well that that fact may be known by the ones chasing you."

Her face became ashen as she sagged against the seat. For a moment, he thought she might swoon. He hoped not, for he had neither *sal volatile* nor burned feathers to revive her. Then he perceived that his concerns were unfounded. Phoebe Brackenton might be scared out of half her wits, but even half of her wits was more than many people had.

"What makes you think anyone is chasing me?" she asked, her voice again studiously calm.

"You were in a ghastly hurry when you jumped into this carriage."

"I was thankful that I had found a way to get back to Mayfair."

"What happened to your carriage?"

She did not hesitate. "I lost it."

"You lost it?" He laughed lowly. "Forgive me, but that is most amusing."

Phoebe found nothing amusing about any of this.

All she wanted was to get home and put this night behind her. In the morning after she was assured that Jasper had made good his escape and was safe, she would try to figure out how to make sense out of this jumble. Stopping her work was not an option, although she was unsure if Jasper or Sam would concur. There had been close calls before, but nothing like tonight.

If they had been betrayed . . . No, she could not think of that.

"It is very easy," she replied, folding her hands in her lap, "to get turned about in the fog."

"That is true."

"I had thought the carriage was in one place, and it turned out not to be."

"So you went looking for it?"

"Yes."

"That seems a reasonable explanation." He settled one booted foot on his opposite knee and relaxed against the seat. "However, I believe you are skirting the truth, Phoebe."

"I don't recall granting you permission to use my given name."

He wagged a finger in front of her. "You are changing the subject. If you wish to remonstrate with me, remember that I am playing your dashing hero tonight, rescuing you from whatever dragon is chasing you." Resting his arm on the back of the seat, he smiled. "Unlike you, I find it easy to fall into bad habits, such as using your given name. Why don't you rectify my sin by using mine?"

"How would that rectify anything?"

"I'm not sure." He laughed. "That is honesty, you must own."

"If it would make you feel better about your *faux pas*, I will do as you ask."

"Are you always so dashed decorous, Phoebe?"

"No."

She could not help smiling when he stared at her as if he could not help himself. Mayhap he had not expected her to be that honest, because he clearly had not believed a word she had spoken until now. She was not certain how to show him that she had been square with him without telling him all that had happened tonight and why.

The hatch opened on the top of the carriage. When she looked up, amazed, the coachee called down, "My lord, we are being followed."

"By whom?" Galen asked.

"I don't recognize the carriage," the coachman replied, "but they are motioning for us to pull over to the side of the road."

"Don't!" Phoebe gasped.

When the viscount's gaze caught hers, she wished she had remained silent. Yet how could she? He leaned toward her, his cape that was as raven as his hair brushing her cloak. With another gasp, she undid the ribbon at her throat and pulled off her own cloak. If she had been followed, she must not let this muddy garment betray her. She balled it up and looked around her. Where could she hide it?

"Allow me," Galen said, holding out his hands.

"Thank you," she whispered. She glanced over her shoulder and out the window at the back of the carriage as she pressed the cloak into his hands. The other vehicle was closing the distance between them.

When his fingers enfolded hers along with the cloak, she looked at him. The light from the lantern might be faint now that her eyes were accustomed to its soft glow, but his eyes burned like two dark fires. That heat surged from his skin through her as he said, "I have no idea what kind of trouble you have gotten yourself into, Phoebe, but, in spite of what you may have heard of me, I am a gentleman, and a gentleman protects any lady in his company."

"Thank you." How many times had she said those words? Many times, but she could not recall a single time when she had meant them more sincerely than she did now.

He opened a drawer under the opposite seat, stuffed the cloak into it, and, as he closed it again, called, "Alfred, pull over and let's see who wants to speak to us so desperately." He peered out of the back of the carriage. "I see two sailors and a man dressed like a gentleman."

"Sailors?"

"Does that mean something to you?"

"There were three sailors on the wharf when I was there, but—" She was saying too much already. Taking a deep breath to steady herself, she rose to her knees to see what he could. He seized her shoulders and pushed her back against the seat.

"Galen!" she cried. "What do you think you are—?"

"Be quiet!" He pressed his hand over her mouth. "Don't say a word."

She peeled his fingers from her lips. "What do—?"

"If you value saving your reputation and anything else you fear for tonight, keep out of sight." He blew out the lantern overhead and motioned for her to remain in the shadows.

She nodded. Mayhap it was some other sailor. There were hundreds in London at any time. Mayhap this was just coincidence. She wished she could believe that.

She peeked out of the back window. There was the filthy sailor Jasper had been speaking with on the wharf! What was he doing here with a man dressed in the finest fashion?

"Do you recognize them?" Galen murmured.

"Yes, one of them."

"Who is he?"

"I can't explain."

"Phoebe—"

When she saw the men walk toward Galen's carriage, she grabbed the lapels of his coat. In the thin light from a streetlamp behind the carriage, she saw his eyes widen in shock before she hid her face against his shoulder. "Pull your cloak around me," she whispered.

He chuckled as he obeyed, his arms enfolding her against him. "As you wish, my lady."

"Draw your cape around both of us," she ordered, wishing almost anyone else had been in this carriage when she climbed into it. She was trembling even more, but it was not only the fear of the sailor now. How could she be so want-witted? When she had last met Galen, his courteous touch had sent delight swirling through her. To be in his arms now . . . She tried to concentrate on what she needed to do so her work could continue uninterrupted.

"Why?"

"I don't want them to recognize me."

He was abruptly somber. "Why?"

"I could be in a great deal of trouble." This was not the time to dissemble.

"When did they last see you?"

"Just before I reached your carriage."

"So that's why you wanted to get rid of your black cloak?"

"Yes, I had it on before so they could not see me in the darkness along the docks."

"You wore it the whole time?"

"Yes."

"The hood, too?"

"As soon as I realized they had seen me." She

glanced back at the carriage behind them, but gasped when her bonnet was plucked from her head. "What are you doing?"

He did not answer as he shoved the bonnet in the drawer with the cloak. She heard the straw crack when he pushed the drawer closed again. Before she could react, he sifted his hands through her hair, loosening it to fall around her shoulders.

"Are you mad?" she asked. "I shall look like a harlot."

"Mayhap I am mad, because I'm trying to help you when I have no idea what sort of bumble-broth you have mixed me up in." Drawing her hair forward over her shoulders, he shook his head. "I hope they did not catch sight of your hair, because it will distinguish you immediately. I've never seen such glorious gold before."

"I—"

"Say nothing." He drew her head back down to his shoulder. His lips brushed her ear as he murmured, "But you need to put your arms around me if you want this to look truly authentic."

"Galen, I believe you are taking advantage of this."

"You may be right." His smile appeared and was gone before she was quite sure she had seen it. "However, you do need my help. So put your arms around me."

Slowly, she lifted her arms to his broad shoulders. The aromas of clean wool and some musky cologne filled every breath. "I want you to know now, in case something goes awry, how I appreciate you helping me."

"Hush," he murmured.

"I want to—" She stared up into his eyes, which were so close to hers. Not even a shadow could have slipped between them. His fingers splayed across her back, keeping her close so she would not look back at the door. He need not have worried, because she doubted she could have looked anywhere but up into his volatile eyes.

"So would I like a few things myself right now, but unfortunately . . ." He turned her face back against his shoulder as he raised his voice. "Good evening, sir. You sailors are quite far from the river. Did you misplace your ship?"

She tensed as the carriage shifted, and she knew someone had put a foot on the step. She wondered if the man was going to open the door and demand that they get out. When Galen's hand patted her back gently, she released the breath she had been holding. She had to trust him now as she had trusted only Sam and Jasper for so long. She hoped he was as worthy of her trust.

"I'm looking for a woman and a man," came an answer in a voice that belonged to the Polite World.

Phoebe breathed a whisper of gratitude. Jasper must be safe!

"You've found one of each." Galen's voice sounded slurred, as if he had been drinking heavily. "What can I do for you, sir?"

"Should call 'im cap'n." At the voice, Phoebe stiffened. She knew it instantly. This *was* the sailor who had been bargaining with Jasper. " 'E's—"

"Cut line," ordered the other man, obviously not wanting to divulge his name. "I'm looking for two people, my lord. One, a man who may have been shot. The woman may have been as well."

Phoebe bit back her gasp when Galen's fingers settled on her leg. Then she realized he was drawing his cape surreptitiously over her gown to hide the bloodstain. What a miracle that she had found such an unexpected ally!

"Haven't seen anything." He gave a hiccup and chortled. "Been too busy with my special friend here."

"Miss?" called the man. "May I ask you what you have seen?"

She turned only far enough to get a glimpse of the man's shadowed features before Galen turned her face back toward him.

"You may not ask her anything." He hiccuped again. "Could cause all kinds of trouble if *he* found out she was with me. Last chap ended up in a duel at Hyde Park. Don't want *him* to pop the fly at me. You understand, don't you?"

The man cleared his throat, embarrassed.

Phoebe's dismay deepened. The man must be of a higher class than the sailor who demanded that he ask her to answer. If a gentleman was involved in trying to halt her, her work must have garnered more attention than she had guessed.

"She's been with you all evening?" the man asked.

"I think so." He gave another drunken laugh. For a long moment, she heard no other sound, then he added in a whisper, his voice once again completely sober, "Don't move yet. They are leaving, but I don't trust them."

"Neither do I."

"Why don't you take the time while we're waiting for them to be on their way to explain what is going on?"

"Galen, I . . ." She closed her eyes and nodded. He had saved her from the ire of the unjust justice of the courts. She owed him the duty of the truth. "I will tell you if you will take me home posthaste to Grosvenor Square."

He nodded. "If you think that is wise."

"I think it is what I must do."

His words, which she had repeated to herself so often in the past five years, released her from the serrated claws of her own fear. Nodding, she sighed. Panic was more dangerous tonight than ever.

"You will have to depend on them to take care of themselves," he murmured as they drove past at a pace that should not draw the men's attention. "I suspect you have trained them for this very emergency."

She nodded, unable to speak as they turned onto a street leading away from the square.

Galen faced her. "If I knew you would be safe, I would take you to my house on Berkeley Square, but I doubt if you'll be safe in London anywhere tonight."

His words sent another chill through her, but she ignored it. Now was not the time to worry about the past. She must think about the future and how she could keep her work from being halted. "If we aren't going to your house, then where are we going?"

"To a friend's home near Bath. It's called Thistlewood Cottage, and I hope it is isolated enough so that we may hide there."

"We?" Horror sank to the very depths of her heart. "You have done nothing wrong."

"No? I was not honest with them when I let them think you were a lady who was having a secret *affaire de coeur* with me."

She reached out to put her hand on his arm, then drew back her fingers. The motion, which would have been so commonplace with anyone else, seemed far too intimate with this man whose very glance unsettled her. "I am so sorry, Galen."

"It is too late for apologies, and you need not apologize. As I told you, it was my decision to help you." When he grinned, she was shocked more than she had been at anything tonight. "This should be fun."

"Fun?"

"Yes. Although the Season is just underway, it seems to be picking up exactly where the last Little Season ended. Mayhap I have come to London for too many Seasons, because all I can see ahead of me here is ennui and playing chaperon for my brother. Helping you should be much more fun."

She stared at him. This was not a game. This was life and death, the lives of those she helped and her death if she were caught. He had to understand that.

"Galen, if you were to be connected with me, you could be ruined or sent to hang with me."

He waved her words aside. "Your warning may be too late, Phoebe. It should not take long for them to connect the lady in my carriage with you. All they need do is look at a portrait of you in your house, and they will know that the beautiful woman in my arms was you. Blast! I should have hidden your hair. I don't want us to be stopped before we can leave London."

"There is no portrait of me in my town house. The only picture is at the house in the country."

He nodded. "We shall send a message from the first coaching inn to have it destroyed immediately."

"My father had it commissioned for him just before he died, and—"

All amusement left his voice as his gaze caught hers again. "I never had the honor of meeting your father, but I cannot help but believe that he would rather have it destroyed than have you dead."

She stared at him as he turned to look out the window. Mayhap she was not the one who was queer in the attic. One minute, Galen Townsend was treating this like a game arranged for his private amusement. The next, he was as serious as a judge pronouncing sentence. Even if he were mad, he was the only ally she had now.

Four

Galen grumbled as a hand shook his shoulder. He would have Roland's head for interrupting his sleep. By Jove, his valet should know better than to wake him when it was not yet light.

His nose twitched. When had Roland taken to wearing such a light cologne? His valet usually smelled of strong soap. This scent delighted every breath he took, urging him to draw in slow, deep ones and fall back into dreams as fragrant. Something struck his face. A woman's bracelet? What was happening?

"Galen! We are stopping!"

That delicate voice was definitely not Roland's, for his valet rumbled like a frog.

"Galen!"

He opened his eyes further. Had his dream been given life? What better way to wake than to find a beautiful woman slanting toward him, her lips soft and inviting him to kiss them? As his fingers sifted up through luxurious golden curls, he smiled.

A hand slapped his, and he yelped. *This* was no dream!

"Galen, will you stop jesting?" Impatience filled the soft voice. "We are slowing. Do you know why?"

"Slowing?" Galen pushed his head up and discov-

ered he had fallen asleep against the wall of his carriage. A cramp in his neck would remind him for hours
to come how stupid he had been to fall asleep here.
Baffled for a moment, he tried to recall why he was
here instead of in his comfortable bed. Rubbing the
back of his neck as he peered out the window, he said,
"We are approaching a village, Phoebe."

"You cannot be thinking of stopping."

He stretched his arms, straining cramped muscles.
When she yelped and knocked away his arm, he said,
"I can see that you are not going to be a good con-
spirator."

"Conspirator? I have no wish to conspire with you."
She huddled into herself. "I want to go home and turn
back the clock so that tonight will never happen."

"A wish I am certain we all have wished one time
or another."

Phoebe looked past him toward where a single light
burned in one building in the midst of the village.
"But never have I worried that because of what I have
done someone might have been killed."

"You said your friend was able to flee."

"Yes, but—"

He took her hand and squeezed it. "You can do no
more now."

"I know."

The carriage rolled to a stop, and Galen opened the
door. He smiled when he saw that the lone light was
set in front of a church. Mayhap Phoebe's luck was
about to take a turn for the better.

"Wait here," he said.

"For what?" Phoebe asked, but Galen was gone so
swiftly that she was unsure if he had heard her question.

She fisted her hands on her lap. She should be
grateful to him for coming to her rescue. She was!

Yet, he seemed to treat the whole of this like a special sport devised for his diversion. It was no game, for people's lives depended on her.

A shudder ached through her. Not only the lives of those on the ships, but now Jasper's and hers.

Closing her eyes, she sighed. Faulting Galen for thinking this was some sort of grand adventure was silly when she had begun it with the same giddy excitement he had now. Then, she had believed that her small efforts would persuade the country's leaders to see the foolishness of the laws that banished someone to the far side of the world for shooting a single rabbit.

Five years had passed, and everything remained the same, save that she might have endangered those who had trusted her the most. Would she ever think with her head instead of her heart?

"Phoebe?"

At Galen's voice, she looked up. Her face must have revealed her thoughts because in the dim light from the lantern hanging by the front door of the church she could see his smile vanish.

He put his hands over hers. "Stay as brave as you have been until now," he said.

"I am not certain if I have been brave or simply foolish."

"I doubt if anyone with a bit of courage has not wondered that once or twice."

Phoebe let him hand her out from the carriage. "If your plan is to leave me here and return to London, let me say I believe you are wise."

"Leave you here?" His brows lowered, adding to the roguish strength of his face. "Why would you think I would do something so untoward? I told you that I would take you to Thistlewood Cottage where you will be safe."

"But you were seeking your brother near the

Thames. I know you must be anxious to assure yourself that he is unharmed."

"I am more anxious to see you safely out of Town where you may hide from those who are chasing you." He pulled off his cape and settled it on her shoulders. Drawing up the collar so it curved along her face, concealing her features, he smiled. "You have trusted your allies, Phoebe. Now you have to trust me."

Phoebe hated the tears that welled into her eyes. She was no wet-goose, but his kindness threatened to undo her completely. "I appreciate this more than I can say."

"Then do as *I* say."

Taken aback by the abrupt change in his tone from gentle to gruff, she nodded. She put her hand on his arm that jutted toward her. When he patted her fingers, she wanted to smile. Her face was too rigid with fear. Why had they stopped here? She wished she had some idea of what he was planning.

Phoebe bit back her questions when he led her around the church toward a small house at the back. She was curious how he had seen it here in the darkness. Mayhap he simply had guessed the pastor's house must be close to the church. He strode up onto the front porch and rapped on the door as if it were the middle of the day. He did not stop knocking until the door was thrown open.

A woman, her nightcap askew, stood in the doorway, trying to hold a candle and close her wrapper at the same time. "Is there an emergency?" she asked.

Galen did not smile. "May we come in and speak of our business in private? I do not want others to overhear."

"That is unlikely at this hour." The woman stepped back. If she took note of Phoebe's stiff feet almost tripping her as she entered the low threshold, she did

not react. Her sleep heavy eyes were aimed at Galen.
They widened when he edged into the narrow circle
of candlelight, standing between the woman and
Phoebe. "Why are you here, sir?"

Instead of correcting how she addressed him, Galen
said, "I would like to speak with the minister of the
church near the road."

"He is not here. He went to call on his sister in
Rochester." The woman set the candle on a table that
had been well polished, for the light reflected back on
them. "I am his housekeeper. Mrs. McBlain."

Galen put his arm around Phoebe's shoulders. When
she was about to shrug it off, she realized he was
pulling up the cloak's collar, so it concealed the side
of her face where the candlelight might reveal her
identity.

"Mrs. McBlain," he replied, "my fiancée and I are
in the midst of our journey from London, and I fear
that she has ruined her clothes."

Phoebe glanced down at her gown that was barely
visible beneath the thick cape. Dirt was caked to the
hem, but no signs of the blood that had stained her
gown were visible. Thank heavens, Galen was thinking
more clearly than she was. She could have betrayed
the truth . . . again.

"And this was one of my favorite frocks, too," she
said, guessing she should say something. A jab in her
side from Galen's elbow sent her breath exploding out
in a puff.

When Mrs. McBlain looked toward her, startled, he
inched forward again a half step and said, "That is
the cost of having a father who does not look kindly
upon her plans to marry." He compressed Phoebe's
hand as he gave her a smile that she guessed he meant
to be romantic, but she found insipid. The message in
his eyes was clear, however. She was to remain silent,

so she did not choose the very words that could bring trouble after them.

Mrs. McBlain clearly found his expression quite believable because she replied, "I take your words to mean you are not looking to marry."

"Not here." He chuckled. "And the way to Gretna Green is long, so you can understand why I wish my beloved to have something less intolerable to wear than clothes that are dirty and torn. I assume the church has a poor box where there are clothing donations."

"For a lady of quality?" Mrs. McBlain's eyes became as round as a child's ball.

"Anything clean will do admirably."

"Simple clothing will be better for our journey," Phoebe said. Again his elbow poked her, warning her to remain silent. Why had he brought her inside if he had not wanted her to speak? To say nothing was certain to create more questions. She was growing more baffled by the moment. She leaned her head on Galen's shoulder, keeping the cloak's collar high, although she was tempted to put her hands around his neck. All of this simply so she could have a clean dress? This was absurd! In a voice as sweet as treacle, she cooed, "I should have trusted you when you advised me of that, darling."

Galen made a low choking sound as if she had truly put her hands around his throat and squeezed. His smile did not waver as he drew some coins from beneath his coat and set them on the table. "I assume this donation will be welcome in exchange for a gown for my beloved."

Looking hastily away, Phoebe wondered how long this charade would continue. She did not like lying to a minister's housekeeper.

"There is a reason for our laws. Folks of good sense

heed them." Mrs. McBlain's expression took on the greedy visage of a cat watching another at a bowl of cream. "The pastor will not be pleased that you are circumventing the laws of England to elope."

Galen placed more coins on the table. "Surely he will understand that love often leads a young couple to make difficult decisions."

"So I have heard." The housekeeper still did not smile.

He set one pound note, then another, then a third next to the coins.

Phoebe bit her lip to keep all her questions unspoken while the housekeeper pocketed the money. When the woman motioned for them to follow, Galen offered his arm again. Phoebe put her hand on it.

"Damn—" He glanced about. "*Dashed* expensive dress from the poor box," he muttered so only she could hear.

She started to reply, but did not when Mrs. McBlain opened a cupboard door and drew out a drawer within it. The housekeeper lifted out two dresses, holding them up in front of Phoebe, who kept her eyes lowered and the cloak closed around her. One was too long, and the other too short. Tossing them back into the box, Mrs. McBlain pulled another from the drawer.

"This should do admirably," the housekeeper said. "It belonged to the squire's daughter, who is of a size with you. She gave some of her clothes to the church when she married Mr. Penney and moved to York."

"Yes," Phoebe said faintly, for she could not imagine wearing the bright green dress that was decorated with blue lace that was even more garish. She would stand out like a midsummer's night fire on a hill.

"What about this?" asked Galen as he reached past the housekeeper and lifted out a gown of a pink that was barely more than white. The fabric was a simple

linen, and the only hint of decoration was a small
white bow in the center of each puffed sleeve.

"Yes," Mrs. McBlain said in a tone that suggested
she wished he had not seen it or that she had asked
him for a larger *donation.* "That looks as if it would
fit you, young lady."

Holding it up against Phoebe, Galen smiled. "And
it looks lovely, my dear."

Phoebe snatched the dress and folded it over her
arm. *My dear!* Galen was relishing this too much. She
did not want to be here watching him act like a ca-
per-wit. This was no lark!

When he thanked Mrs. McBlain, Phoebe echoed his
words and turned to walk back out toward the carriage.
She saw a pair of forms near it, but only Galen's
coachee was waiting when they reached it. Mayhap
her eyes had betrayed her. As exhausted as she was,
for she had not slept well last night in anticipation of
going to the Pool before the *Trellis* sailed for Australia,
she could not depend on what her eyes were showing
her.

She yawned when they reached the road in front of
the church. Lamps were now lit in several of the
houses on the far side of what she now saw was a
small green. Instead of looking at the houses, she
turned toward the road leading to London. She wished
she could sprout wings and fly back there to discover
what had happened after Galen's coachee had applied
the whip to the horses.

"You have your allies trained well, I am sure,"
Galen said as he came to stand behind her. "Trust
them to do what they must until you can get back to
London."

"I must," she said, not surprised that he could guess
the course of her thoughts.

"Trust them or go back?"

"Both." She faced him. "You lie easily."

"Quite to the contrary." He handed her into the carriage. "I prefer honesty in all my dealings. However, I know duplicity is necessary now."

Glancing toward the houses that were lit, she asked, "Why are we remaining here? Are we going on tonight?"

"Be patient," he said with another chuckle. "I want to give Alfred some instructions for the next part of our trip."

"Ask him as well to whom he was speaking while we were in the minister's house."

"Speaking to?"

"I believe I saw someone speaking with your coachee when we came out of the house."

He gave her a smile. "Who would be up at this hour to speak with Alfred?"

"I don't know. That is what I hoped you could find out."

"I shall check with him. Relax, Phoebe."

Wanting to tell him he was wasting his breath, that relaxing was as impossible as her flying back to Town, Phoebe sagged back against the seat. She should be grateful to him for all he was doing for her. Yet she wanted to ask him why he was doing all this. His actions contrasted with his reputation as a man who basked in all the entertainments available in London.

Or mayhap this all did make sense. He seemed to find the whole of this—and her—most entertaining.

Galen came to the carriage door and reopened it. "We are set to leave."

"Who was speaking with Alfred?"

"He suspects you saw motion from the horses and mistakenly thought it was a person."

Phoebe said nothing when he climbed into the carriage and sat beside her. She wanted to believe him, but she had to believe her own eyes. Or could she? Mayhap exhaustion was tempting her to give into fear.

She took off Galen's cloak. Folding it, she set it and the dress between them on the seat. He glanced down at the clothes and gave a hushed chuckle. If he thought to provoke her into speaking, he was going to fail.

The carriage began moving again, and Galen stretched out his legs as far as he could in the cramped carriage. He rested his arm on the back of the seat as he said, "You look bothered, Phoebe."

"I am." She was astonished how pleased she was that he had broken the silence.

"Because you think I am bereft of my senses."

She wished she could see his face, but it was lost in the shadows. "Mrs. McBlain will most definitely remember us stopping there."

"True."

"If we are followed—"

"That is why I did not give the good reverend's housekeeper either of our names."

"But if she describes us, we could be stopped before we get to Thistlewood Cottage."

"She will not be able to describe you, because I made sure I stood between the light and you whenever possible."

"She saw you."

He laughed. "Even so, no one will expect that you and I are together. We have seldom spoken when among the *ton*. If someone is chasing after this carriage, they have no reason to connect the woman I am supposedly eloping with is Lady Phoebe Brackenton." He laughed again as leaned toward her. "Already I have given your pursuers reason to believe I am madly in love with a woman whose face, if revealed, could create all kinds of a to-do among the elite."

"You are having too much fun with this."

"Fun? I must own it will be great fun that in no time the Polite World will be buzzing with the *on dits* of Lord Townsend and how that blackguard has persuaded some miss to believe that he would marry her when they ran off together to daisyville."

Phoebe smiled. "You are more than a bit diabolical in your schemes."

"Yes, I think I may be." His arm curved down over her shoulder as he tilted her head onto his. Although she could not see his face, she recalled how his eyes had twinkled when she first spoke to him in Lady Beterley's foyer. With the same hint of humor that had filled his voice that night, he added, "But now it is time to get some sleep. Shall we sleep together here?"

She sat up straight. "Are you mad?"

"No, simply exhausted." He shrugged. "If you do not wish to sleep, Phoebe, I beg your indulgence, for I am ready to journey off to the land of nod." He kissed her lightly on the cheek.

"Really, Galen! Kissing me!" Outraged, she turned her back on him and stared out the other window.

When her shoulders were taken, she gasped as he twisted her back to face him. All mirth had vanished from his voice when he said, "If you think that *really* was a kiss, I could show you how mistaken you are."

She lifted his hands off her shoulders and shoved them away. "If you think this is funny, then you are the one who is mistaken. Save your *bon mots* for Almack's, my lord. I have neither the inclination nor the time for them."

Phoebe slid as close to the wall of the carriage as she could. Letting her shoulders slump again, she stared out at the stars that were being consumed by a bank of clouds. The silence within the carriage rumbled in her ears more loudly than the sound of the wheels on the uneven road. The weight of all that had happened in the past day ground down onto her head, making it ache as if the carriage had ridden over her.

She slowly clenched her hands, longing to hear Galen speak to her, to apologize or to comfort her or even to fire another comment at her again.

When she heard his breathing slow, she closed her eyes. She had never felt so lost and alone.

Five

Galen picked his way across the muddy yard of the inn. The carriage was not as badly damaged as he had feared when they had almost lost a wheel in a rut. Only the skill of his coachee, Alfred, had kept the carriage from tipping over.

As it was, a pain slashed Galen's right elbow each time he moved his arm. He suspected Phoebe had injured her left ankle, although she said she was unhurt, because she had been limping when he helped her out of the carriage. She had tried to hide her uneven steps from him, but he had been watching closely.

His smile returned. He liked watching her walk. The sway of her skirt was as assertive as her belief that she could bring about a change in the country's laws with her simple act of defiance. Mayhap if he had not indulged himself in observing her as much, he would have missed seeing the slight unsteadiness in her steps.

When his foot hit a broken wooden bucket that careened ahead of him, Galen paid more mind to where he was walking. He could barely see in the deepening twilight. He would have preferred driving to a better inn, but this one was the closest. Alfred had needed every bit of his skill in the box to get them this far, and Galen had not wanted to chance the carriage on unfamiliar roads in the dark.

"How is the carriage? Is it repairable?" asked Phoebe as he came up the stairs to the wide porch.

He took her arm and steered her with cautious, slow steps toward the inn's door and away from the eager eyes of the men who were loitering in front of the porch, talking about the day's work. "Why are you remaining outside? You should have gotten somewhere out of sight as quickly as you could."

"I did not want to come inside alone."

Galen was about to remonstrate with her again, then looked around the interior of the inn. It consisted of one large public room and a passage that vanished into the shadows. The stone floor had not been washed recently, even though there were pools of liquid in every depression. He decided it was wiser not to try to determine what they were.

"Alfred said he should have the carriage fixed by morning," he said.

"By morning? You expect me—I mean, you expect us to stay in this place tonight?"

"Where else? The stables?"

"They can hardly be worse," she said with a shudder.

Galen laughed tightly. "You can say that simply because you haven't seen them." He raised his voice as the shadows became a form. "Good evening, sir."

The dark-haired innkeeper eyed them both, appraising the value of their clothes, no doubt. With Galen's cloak hiding Phoebe's once-elegant gown, the short man would not be able to guess she was a lady fleeing the authorities.

"We need a place in which to stay tonight," Galen said quietly.

"For you and the missus?" the innkeeper asked in a low grunt.

"Yes."

Phoebe stared at Galen, wondering if he had lost what little sense he had left. For a man who professed that he would rather speak the truth, he was telling too many out-and-outers.

"This way," said the innkeeper, holding his hand out as he named the price for the room.

Galen dropped several coins in the man's hand, then put his arm around Phoebe to steer her after the innkeeper. "Don't even say it," Galen murmured.

"Say what?" She concentrated on trying to keep as much weight as possible off her left ankle. If she was not careful, the tiny twinge became a piercing pain.

"That you intend to repay me as soon as you can," he replied.

She wondered how many more ways he could discern her thoughts and still miss so many. Yes, she had wanted to tell him last night that she would repay him—eventually—for the money he had given Mrs. McBlain, as well as the food he had bought for them earlier today.

"It is not necessary," he said in the same near whisper as they walked through a narrow, twisting corridor that was lit by two windows that gave a view of a kitchen garden. It might be neat or filled with weeds, for the darkness hid most of it.

"I do like to even my debts," she replied softly.

"It seems as if you are in the business of balancing debts, and that is what has gotten you into such a shocking mull."

Phoebe did not answer as the innkeeper opened a door and said, "First door on the left, sir."

She stared at the dimly lit staircase behind the door.

She bit back her moan at the thought of climbing it when her ankle was so sore.

A bit of the sound must have escaped because Galen said, "Let me help."

"I should be fine."

"I would like to help."

She nodded, not wanting to get into a brangle with him when the innkeeper was avidly listening to each word they spoke. When Galen bent to lift her up into his arms, she saw anguish slip across his face.

"I can get up the stairs on my own," she whispered, too aware of the innkeeper watching.

"Now that I have you here, don't move. It will irritate my elbow more." He began up the narrow stairs.

Leaning her head against his chest, so she would not bang it on the wall, she said, "You are being jobbernowl to carry me like this when you are going to exacerbate the injury that clearly has been done to your arm."

"I told you that I shall be fine as long as you do not move."

"Are you certain that you shall be fine?"

He stepped up into the passage at the top of the stairs and carried her through an open door. Shoving the door closed with his foot, he gave her the rakish smile that she guessed had melted many hearts before hers. Icy dismay clutched her anew when he laughed and said, "Holding you makes me feel very, very fine, Phoebe."

"Has anyone told you that you are incorrigible?"

"A few people."

"How about irritating?"

"A few more."

"And vexing?"

"Yes, they have told me that as well as informing

me that I can be exasperating and incomprehensible and simply bothersome."

When he set her on the bed, which was the only piece of furniture beneath the room's slanting ceiling, save for a washstand where a single candle burned, she bounced to her feet. A moan burst from her as she foolishly put weight onto her ankle.

"You would be wiser to sit and not hurt yourself," Galen said, loosening his cravat. "You must own that it would be better for my arm not to have to tote you back down the stairs on the morrow."

"There will be no need for you to do so." She undid his cloak and draped it over the footboard. On top of it, she placed the dress he had pulled out of the poor box for her. She longed to have a chance to get clean and put it on.

He faced her and smiled. "You should not get in such a pelter, Phoebe, simply because I gave you a kiss on the cheek."

"It was a most unseemly thing to do," she answered, glad that they finally were speaking of what had happened last night. In such a short time, Galen had become a necessary part of her life. She did not want him angry at her, because she was not sure when she might have to trust him as completely as she did the others who helped her.

"Odd, for, to me, it seemed the proper thing to do when you were obviously so distressed." He closed the distance between them with one step.

When she backed away, she bumped her head on the low ceiling. "Very well. I shall accept your apology, and we shan't speak of this again."

"Apology? I do not recall apologizing."

"I thought . . ." Phoebe took a deep, steadying breath. "You are the most annoying man I have ever met."

"Ah, I have heard other people say that as well."
He sat on the edge of the bed. "And you are proving
to be more interesting all the time, Phoebe."

"Interesting?"

He smiled at her. "The Lady Phoebe I had heard
discussed during various assemblies was always lauded
as a woman who was quiet and kept much to herself.
There was some question if she might be an unre-
deemable bluestocking who had no interest in the
gatherings of the *ton,* for she often left them not soon
after she arrived."

"People have said that?" She pressed her hand over
her heart, which faltered in midbeat. "I had no idea
that anyone had taken note of my leaving."

"Each member of the *ton* notices everything in
hopes of learning something of interest before someone else does. That you have slipped away more than
once without explanation seems to have caught several
eyes." His grin became mischievous. "Do you wish
to know where they think you are going?"

"Your expression suggests it is a place that a lady
should not speak of."

"A lover's arms is a place many ladies speak of."

"Oh." Heat soared up her face.

"You cannot let your chagrin at breaking the law
persuade you that others might have guessed the truth.
I must own, Phoebe, that, at first, I had assumed you
were fleeing from some lover when you abducted me
along with my carriage. I could not guess another reason you might be out at midnight in such a place."

"That is a relief." She started to smile, but her smile
vanished when he drew her down to sit beside him.
When she would have jumped to her feet, horrified
to be perched on a bed with a man who was little
more than a stranger—and a notorious one at that—he

kept her next to him. His strong arm curved around her waist.

When his fingers encountered a rip in the side of her gown, they slipped into it. Fear erupted through her. He had been a gentleman when they were in London. Recalling the stories she had heard of his dalliances with other women, she berated herself as a goose. He might only have agreed to bring her from Town so he could treat her with such boorishness.

"Galen, stop!"

"Stop? I have not started anything."

"You are being overly presumptuous!"

His brows shot up. "In what way?"

"What do you mean?"

"I mean just what I said." His lips twitched. "Just what I asked."

She plucked his fingers away from her. "I think you are pushing the bounds of propriety by reaching beneath my gown." Fire scored her face at her own crude words.

"Beneath your gown? I would never presume to treat a lady so."

"But your fingers were here where no gentleman's would be." She pointed to the tear in her dress.

His eyes widened, then he chuckled. "What is your dress made of, Phoebe?"

"Silk."

"And your undergarments?" He laughed again. "Do not blush at such a prosaic question."

"It is an impertinent question."

"Mayhap, but I do believe I have a right to ask it when you have already labeled me a scoundrel and have given me not the slightest chance to defend myself."

"You are glib, my lord."

"And you are avoiding giving me an answer, my

lady. Could it be because you realize that you have misjudged me? That because both your gown and your undergarment are made of silk, what you called my presumptuous action was nothing more than an innocent error."

She lowered her eyes. "Forgive me. You are quite right."

He put his arm around her again, cupping her chin with his other hand. Slanting toward her, he murmured, "Trust me, Phoebe. If it had been anything other than a mistake, you would not have been the only one who was aware of where my fingers were."

"You should not speak so. Even in jest."

" 'Twas no jest. You are a beautiful woman. What man can resist playing your hero?"

"I do owe you a debt, Galen, for all you have done for me."

Instantly he drew back, but kept his arm around her shoulder. "Is obligation the only reason you let me hold you even this chastely?"

"Should there be another? I barely know you, and I do not make it a habit to be found in strangers' arms. Let me go, please."

"You are the one who said I am no gentleman, Phoebe."

"You certainly are no gentleman if you taunt me when I am fearful about what has happened to my household."

"To own the truth, at a time like this, when I am with a beautiful woman in an inn beyond the environs of London, I should be kissing her warm lips." When she gasped at his brazen words, he added, "However, you do not need to be fearful. I assure you, that despite your fears to the contrary, I am very much of a gentleman, and you shall leave this inn with your virtue intact."

When he chuckled, her face became stiff with fury. She should have heeded the tales she had heard about him and spun him a tale of a tryst gone bad. Then he would have taken her home to Grosvenor Square and taken his leave.

Phoebe shivered at that thought. If she had been at home when those three men who had been chasing called, she was not sure what would have happened. She had talked herself out of difficult situations since she had embarked on this attempt to save those who had done so little wrong. She had to be grateful that Galen had been so nice as to offer her a way to flee.

From under her lowered eyelashes, she regarded him. No, nice was not the word for Galen Townsend. With his eyes that missed nothing around him, he reminded her of the sleek tiger cat that ruled the barn on her family's country estate. The cat never tried to subdue those around him with his claws, but all knew under his purring, self-satisfied exterior was a fierce fighter that would protect his domain. The comparison made her even more uncomfortable.

Galen stood.

She looked up at him, wrenched from her uneasy thoughts. "Are you going somewhere?"

"I thought I might find something for us to eat while you take a nap."

"I am not sleepy."

"Not sleepy?" He frowned as his hands settled on her shoulders. "If I did not know you better, I would say you were quite mad, Phoebe."

"Know me better? You do not know me at all!"

"I suspect I know you better than most people do, because you have divulged to me the most precious secrets you keep in your heart." He smiled. "That is why I know you should get some rest now while you can."

"I cannot sleep." She came to her feet. "I am too worried about my friends. I know Johnson—"

"Who?"

"My butler Johnson. He would have answered the door to those three beastly men."

"You are worrying needlessly about your allies. They should be quite safe because without you, there is no proof of any wrongdoing."

"That is true. Why have I not thought of that?"

"Because you have not slept in two days."

"I cannot when I worry so for them. It is an unending circle I cannot escape."

"If you do not sleep, you will make a mistake."

Phoebe limped to the room's single window. She opened it, but odors from the open sewer at the back of the inn shoved through. Closing it again, she sighed. "I have already made a terrible mistake, Galen. If I had trusted Jasper to handle those men alone, he might not have been hurt and those we had planned to help would be on their way somewhere safe in England."

"Have you considered how many times you have eluded trouble and assisted those who had no one else to turn to?" His voice warned he was right behind her. Before she had a chance to react, he turned her to face him. With a single fingertip, he tipped her chin up so her gaze met his. "And how many you hope to help in the future?"

"Why are you helping *me*?" she whispered. "Your title will offer you no more protection than mine."

"I cannot keep from admiring you for doing what you believe is right, even though everyone else would condemn you."

"As you do with your brother?"

He recoiled as if she had struck him. When she put her hand out to him, he walked back to sit on the bed.

Her outstretched fingers curled into a fist, and she slowly lowered it to her side.

"I should not repeat gossip I have heard either," Phoebe said, hobbling back the few steps to where he sat. "I know how many untruths there are amidst the hints of truth."

"But the fact that my brother is worrisome to me is true."

She knelt beside where he was sitting, trying not to groan as she moved her leg. "I am sorry to bring up this subject which clearly bothers you."

"It is not easy to be thought of as addle-witted."

"Kindness is never addle-witted."

"The exact response I would have expected from you." His voice took on a jaunty tone as he said, "I am hungry, but I do not wish to go downstairs and leave you alone while you change."

"What?"

He pointed to the door. "The latch on that would be easily overmastered by anyone intent on getting in here. I doubt you would be interested in meeting an intruder while you are dressed in your smallclothes." A devilish twinkle came into his eyes. "Your *silk* smallclothes."

"You expect me to change while you are in the room?"

He went to the window. "If you blow out the candle, you can change in the corner beside the bed. I do not have a cat's eyes, so you need not worry about me seeing through the dark." He turned to look out the window. "My eyes will not shift from this charming view of the stableyard."

"You could go——"

"Where? Downstairs? Even if I were willing to leave you alone here, do you want to create more gossip, Phoebe, by having me wandering about the inn while my supposed wife is changing?"

She sniffed. "Now there was a poor idea."

"What was a poor idea?"

"Telling the innkeeper that you were my husband. That was a poor idea."

"Do you think so?" He crossed the room toward her, his boots striking the floor sharply on each step. "I thought it would be much less remarkable if a gentleman sought a room for his wife to rest in while the carriage was repaired than to let our host believe we were seeking privacy for an illicit tryst."

"Really, Galen!"

"Do not tell me that you are embarrassed by such plain speech. Surely you have heard its like and far worse during your visits to . . ." He smiled abruptly, but there was no warmth in his expression.

"You are right. I have heard its like and far worse, but I do not ever find it pleasant."

He laughed and sat once more on the bed. Folding his arms on the simple footboard, he shifted one arm. She wondered how badly he had hurt it when the carriage had nearly turned over. He rested his chin on left arm and looked up at her. "How have you managed to do this for so many years and still maintain this gentility?"

"What I do to save a few families does not change who I am."

"No?"

"I would like to think not." She rubbed her hands together. "Yet I am certain I have been changed in so very many ways. This all started because my heart was broken for one family. Now I am so deep into it that I am unsure I could stop, even if I wished to."

"And do you wish to?"

"No! For each person I help, there are scores more

who are just as innocent of a heinous crime but are unable to get off the ships."

"So you will continue with this once the furor dies down?"

"What choice do I have?"

"The same choice you have always had. To continue or to stop."

She touched the stains on her gown. "There is only one real choice. I must continue."

Six

The sun had set hours before, slipping into view from behind a bank of clouds that threatened more rain, but Galen had not called a halt to the day's journey. After the disgusting place where they had spent last night, he wanted to be sure that tonight the inn where they stopped offered clean bedding and a decent meal.

"And some ale that does not taste like thin broth," he muttered to himself.

Hearing a murmur from beside him, he looked over to see if his hushed words had roused Phoebe. She had lost her fight to remain awake about two hours ago, which was another reason he had let Alfred continue driving along the road leading into the sunset.

He smiled. Phoebe's eyes were still closed, so she must have been talking in her sleep. Were her dreams haunted by what had sent her fleeing into his carriage?

Leaning back, he stared up at the carriage's roof. What had seemed like the best solution to an intolerable problem was proving to be insufferable as well. He had forgotten how the featherbed lanes between London and Bath left every bone jostled and aching.

He cursed when the front left wheel bounced into a chuckhole. That was the one that had been damaged yesterday. The carriage needed only to hold together until they could reach Hamdenford, which should be the next village. The lad had said he could ride to Bath and deliver Galen's orders in ripping time, so a carriage from Thistlewood Cottage should be waiting at the inn there.

Voices of a choir practicing pulled Galen from his doze. He realized the carriage was slowing to a stop. Looking across the carriage at Phoebe, he saw she was still asleep, her hand curled under her cheek. The dress from the poor box did not fit her well, but the color flattered her.

His fingers longed to stroke her soft skin as he woke her with an eager kiss. How many other women had he teased with kisses that meant less than the bubbles in a glass of champagne? He was surprised that he could not recall the last one. Watching over his brother had kept him too busy for the past few months to enjoy a few escapades of his own.

Hearing the echo of his brother's laughter, Galen knew what Carr would say about this gallant effort to save Phoebe Brackenton. Carr would have given him a dressing-down for risking his life for a stranger. For a moment, Galen envied his brother's focus only on himself.

Galen stepped out of the carriage as soon as it came to a complete stop. Looking at the inn, he smiled. It was cleaner than where they had stayed last night, and the aromas coming from it did not threaten to create an upheaval in his stomach.

Hearing a creak from the carriage, he said, "Alfred, despite all odds, we have made it this far."

"Yes, my lord." He jumped down from the box.

"Thanks to you, the carriage lasted until we reached Hamdenford. Will you be able to get it back to London to be repaired?"

Alfred nodded his grizzled head. "I believe so, although I shall have to go even more slowly than we did today."

Galen chuckled. "I suspect you were much bothered this afternoon at the thought that the lad and his flock of sheep might pass us by."

"I was."

Slapping his coachee on the shoulder, Galen said, "I shall tell the innkeeper to make sure that you are served the best ale he has."

"Thank you, my lord." He hesitated, then glanced inside the carriage. "She is asleep, I see."

"At last."

"Odd sort of lady, if you do not mind me saying so."

"Not as long as she does not hear you say so." He laughed quietly.

Alfred's eyes grew wide. "My lord, I would never speak so in a lady's hearing." He faltered, then asked, "Do you wish me to help get her into the inn?"

"She weighs less than Carr. If I can lift him into the carriage when he is completely foxed, I can lift her out."

Alfred nodded. "I do not doubt that, my lord." He walked back to check the horses.

Galen watched his coachee for a long minute. Alfred thought Galen had lost every bit of sense he had ever possessed. The coachman could be correct. Leaving Town and his responsibilities on this madcap race to protect Phoebe had been the most absurd thing he had ever done, but he still could not see, even looking back at the events, how he would have done anything differently. He could not have handed her over to those men who were chasing her.

He slipped his arms beneath Phoebe and gently lifted her from the carriage. Shifting her against him, he cursed under his breath as the toe of her shoe struck his knee even as his motion created a new cascade of pain from his accursed elbow. He shook his head when Alfred turned to ask him a question. Waking Phoebe now would create another flurry of questions that he was too tired to answer.

Galen realized how exhausted Phoebe must be when she did not wake while he spoke to a round, dark-haired woman who greeted him at the door.

"Ah, the poor lamb is deep asleep," cooed the woman who had introduced herself as Mrs. Chester, the innkeeper's wife.

He nodded.

"Come this way," Mrs. Chester said. "I have a lovely room that will be just perfect for you."

When Mrs. Chester opened the door, Galen gave her a quiet request for some food to be prepared for them and also to send out a mug of ale and a plate to Alfred. The innkeeper's wife smiled so broadly that Galen had the suspicion she wanted to pinch him on the cheek as if he were a lad.

He went into the room, taking care that neither Phoebe's head nor her feet struck the door frame. The room was simple, the furniture spare. Candles burned on the small tables set beneath the window. He gave the chamber only a cursory glance as he walked to the bed.

His breath burned beneath his heart, which seemed to be pounding through every inch of him as he imagined carrying her into his own bedchamber where the bed was wide and draped in green velvet. Looking down at her face softened in sleep and resting against his shoulder, he thought of how it would be to hold her through the rest of the night. The slow rise and fall of her breasts brushed against him, and her fingers rested against the center of his chest. He wanted them touching him far more intimately as he sampled every bit of her.

Galen came to his senses from the enchantment she had woven around him even while asleep. Angrily, he berated himself. Phoebe Brackenton was not a harlot who promised a night's entertainment in exchange for the proper payment. She had set aside her life of wariness to trust him. He could not betray her at the very first opportunity.

Yet he was unable to keep himself from looking at where her gown had drifted back to reveal her lithe legs encased in silk stockings. He cursed under his breath and forced his gaze away from that enticing view. Instead he stared at the hard chair by the hearth. At least one of them had a chance to get a good night's sleep.

He placed her gently on the bed. She murmured something he could not understand as he removed her shoes. He was glad to see her ankle was not swollen. Pulling the covers over her, he bent and brushed her tawny hair from her face. When he kissed her soft cheek, her light breaths of sleep caressed him, urging him to taste her lips.

She was such a contradiction. A child-woman. Winsome and sensual, delightfully laughing and haughtily chill, braver than anyone he had ever met and yet frightened by her own passions.

"Sleep well, Phoebe," he whispered as he took the pillow from the other side of the bed and picked up a quilt waiting on a rack. He tossed them both onto the hard chair before blowing out the candle. He closed the door and locked it behind him, knowing she would haunt his dreams tonight. Even as he walked down the steps to deal with a matter that could not wait, he was hoping that he was in hers.

That was madness, he knew, but everything seemed

a bit off-kilter now. And he was relishing it more than he had anything since . . . since his brother had taken ill, and Galen had been consumed by the task of making sure his brother did not do something so stupid again.

Had Carr been found and taken home? Galen wished he knew the answer to that. If his brother lingered in the low taverns along the Pool, Carr was guaranteed to get himself in such a pickle he might not be able to extricate himself from the situation.

Galen kneaded his aching elbow as he walked to where Alfred was sitting on the ground by the carriage. The coachee wiped foam off his mouth as he took another deep drink. When Alfred started to come to his feet, Galen motioned for him to remain where he was.

Perching on the step to the carriage, Galen looked around to be certain no one else was nearby. He smiled when Alfred held up the mug. Galen took a drink and handed it back to his coachee.

"When you get back to London, have clothes for Lady Phoebe sent to Thistlewood Cottage," Galen said.

"Where is that, my lord?"

"Don't worry about that. Deliver her things to Sir Ledwin Woods in Kensington High Street. He will know where to send them." Galen bent toward his coachee and lowered his voice. "Say nothing to Sir Ledwin about what is in the box or by whom it will be received. Let him know only that I want the box brought to Thistlewood Cottage."

"I will say nothing to Sir Ledwin. Should I be as reticent to Lady Phoebe's servants?"

"Her servants? Why would you be speaking with them?"

Alfred reached under his mud-splattered coat. "She gave me this note to be delivered to—"

"By Lord Harry, I know she has more sense than a goose, but she is trying to prove me wrong!" He held out his hand. "Let me see it."

"Yes, my lord." There was clear reluctance in Alfred's voice as he handed the single sheet to Galen.

Slipping the folded page beneath his own coat, Galen sighed. "I know you feel you are breaking a promise you made to the lady."

"Yes, my lord."

"Then let me make a promise to you. I promise that this note will be delivered as it should be. It cannot be taken to her house by someone who can be connected to me, for that might undo all we are trying to do. Whatever you do, do not go near Lady Phoebe's house yourself. Make sure that the request for her clothes is handled without anyone being the wiser. You can trust her butler. I believe she mentioned last night that his name is Johnson. Be certain the request is handed only to him. It would not be in her best interests if some other man found out where she is just now."

"Some other gentleman?"

"I would not call him a gentleman." Galen chuckled, knowing that was the truth. He had not recognized the man with the churlish sailors, for the night had concealed the man's face as completely as it had Phoebe's. He had tried to connect the man's voice with someone he knew but had failed. Mayhap the fine-talking man had just been a more cultured thief-taker.

Thief-taker! If the Bow Street Runners were in pursuit of Phoebe, she must be doubly wary. Those chaps had a way of finding the most cunning criminals. No, the man could not be a Bow Street Runner, because the sailor had called him "Cap'n."

"Ah, I understand," Alfred said, bringing Galen's attention back to his man. "The chap must be a varlet to create all this trouble for my lady."

"He is trouble, that is for certain." He looked up as a drop of rain struck him. Dash it! He needed to make Alfred understand the gravity of the circumstances they were in. "That is why I want you to have the request for her things delivered to Lady Phoebe's house by someone who cannot be connected to me or to her."

"It won't be easy."

"I trust that you will find a clever way to accomplish this."

Alfred scratched the back of his neck and took another drink of his ale. "As you wish, my lord. I shall try."

Galen stood and walked back toward the porch of the inn, ducking his head into the rain that splattered the yard. Alfred thought he was queer in the attic to be making such requests. Mayhap if he had taken Alfred into his confidence right from the start . . . Impossible! Better to let his coachee believe that Phoebe was fleeing an overly amorous lover than for anyone else to know the truth.

"Is everything as you hoped it would be, sir?" asked the innkeeper's wife, who must keep a close eye on the door and her guests.

"Yes." He did not slow his stride as he walked past the public rooms to where he had left Phoebe sleeping. Then he turned and went back into the cozy room where the innkeeper, a ruddy-featured man, was pouring ale into tankards.

Taking one, Galen nodded to his host and took a deep drink. He carried the tankard to a table in the corner farthest from the hearth, not wanting to intrude on the cards that were being played in front of it. One of the trio of men called out, asking if he wanted to join them.

"No thank you, friend," Galen replied.

The man shrugged and bent back over his flats. He tossed a coin onto the pile between the three men.

Galen sat and opened the note. Phoebe's handwriting was not as neat and precise as he had expected. Then he realized that she must have written it in the carriage while he was slumbering. Even though the letters bounced across the page as the carriage had along the road, he could pick out the words easily.

Johnson,

The situation with my latest call has taken a turn for the worse. I trust Jasper found his way back to the house and that you have had him tended to. Do not worry on my behalf. I am fine. I will return to London as soon as the situation with my most recent call eases enough to allow that.

Galen grinned wryly. If he had not known better, he would have guessed, upon reading this, that she had done nothing worse than commit an unforgivable *faux pas* at some assembly. She was now a master of duplicity.

Yet she possessed an innocence that contrasted with the deception she was perpetuating with this note to her butler. He finished the rest of his ale, wadded up the note, and walked to the hearth. Throwing the note onto the fire, he smiled. He had promised that the note would be delivered as it should be. And this was where it belonged.

Galen went to the room he had rented. Pulling out the key, he unlocked the door as quietly as he could. He did not want to wake Phoebe, for she had spent too many hours without sleep. He stifled a yawn. During the hectic swirl of the Season, he had often gone a couple of days before he sought his bed. He had not guessed that sitting in a carriage, constantly looking over his shoulder, would leave him more exhausted than forty unbroken hours of playing cards at his club.

He swore under his breath when a pain rushed up his arm from his elbow. If he had let Alfred help him bring Phoebe in here this evening, he might not have reinjured it. That was his reward for playing a hero. But at least she had stayed lost in her dreams.

Pulling off one boot, then the other, he cursed again when the familiar motion brought on the all-too-familiar flare up along his arm. He set them at the foot of the bed. One slipped from his hands and struck the floor sharply. Straightening, he looked over the footboard, hoping he had not awakened Phoebe.

The bed was empty.

Where was she?

"Are you looking for me, Galen?" came a sleepy voice from the corner.

He lit the candle and frowned when he saw Phoebe propped up in the chair, her feet tucked beneath her and her hand beneath her cheek as it had been in the carriage. He gasped, unable to halt himself. Was she bereft of her wits? "What are you doing *there?*"

"I thought you would sleep better on the bed. After all, you slept on the floor last night."

"But you are—"

She frowned at him. "Galen, I appreciate your gallantry, but I need you wide-awake and able to do what you must to make sure we reach this haven you have promised me. Do not use the argument that, as a gentleman, you should endure all the discomfort."

"It is a gentleman's obligation."

"You have obligations enough without me adding to the weight of your burdens."

"What does that mean?"

She sat up and looked at him through sleep-heavy eyes. "That, since he almost died, your brother is—"

"My brother?" His eyes narrowed as his brows lowered. "It seems that you have listened to gossip more than you led me to believe."

"Nonsense. I listened to Alfred."

"Alfred? What else has he spoken to you of beyond the weather and the conditions of the horses . . . and Carr?"

Drawing her feet up onto the chair again, she stated, "You should not accuse either me or your coachman of gossiping."

"Then how did you know about Carr?"

"I may not gossip, Galen, but I cannot avoid hearing it. Half of the Polite World is agog with his adventures in the lowest taverns. The other half is amused by how you are trying to halt them from continuing."

"Amused?"

She did not lower her gaze. "You must have heard the poker-talk as well."

"Enlighten me."

"I would rather not."

"It is the least you could do."

Phoebe flinched at his acidic tone. She had not intended to send Galen up into the boughs, but her tired brain had not kept her from saying what she should have not. "Yes, it is, I suppose."

He sat on the bed, facing her. "Enlighten me."

"It is said that you are a prime rake."

"That is about me, not about my brother."

Phoebe stood, wishing she could shake him and get him to lose that cool expression that suggested he was as heartless as some *on dits* suggested. "Galen, I do not like repeating gossip."

"Then speak it but once, and I shall listen."

For a moment, she hoped he was hoaxing her, but she saw he was not. "Very well. I heard it said at Lord Litten's house last week that you watch over your brother more closely than an old tough guards her young charge."

"And?"

"That you are wasting your time, for he is doomed to find trouble, no matter what you do."

He came to his feet and clasped his hands behind his back. He let his hands fall to his sides as he winced. Because of his elbow or because of his reaction to her words?

"I intend," he said coolly, "to prove to all the Polite World that they are wrong in that opinion." He stepped closer to her. "Do you believe what they say?"

"I told you that gossip does not interest me. Your brother is your concern, Galen, while my activities are mine."

"Activities? You make it sound so innocent."

"It is when innocent people are being punished so harshly."

"They are not completely innocent."

Phoebe let her shoulders ease from her stiff pose. "No, not completely innocent, but surely not deserving of such a punishment." She stepped away from him. "I do not wish to speak of that or of your brother. We are both too tired to be thinking clearly."

"You are right."

"I am glad you agree."

His arm went around her waist, and he tugged her up against his chest. "I would not do this if I was thinking clearly."

His mouth slanted across hers as his fingers curved

up her back. Her hands rose to push him from her, for she should chide him for being so forward, but somehow they found their way around his shoulders instead. A fire burst forth within her as she dissolved within his luminous kiss. When his mouth slipped along her neck, the aroma of the ale he had been drinking rushed over her, sweeter than any perfume. As her fingers dipped beneath his high collar to curve along his nape, he captured her mouth again.

"No," she whispered as she drew away from him. "This will only complicate everything more."

"Yes, it will." He traced her lower lip that was tender from his feverish kiss.

"I already have too many complications in my life." She took another step back, then gripped the foot of the bed as her ankle protested.

"I will not kiss you again tonight if you agree to one thing."

"What is that?"

"That you will sleep in the bed."

"Galen! You tricked me!"

"I did. So do you agree?"

"Yes."

He gave her a wry smile. "I was afraid you would say that. I have to own that I never thought I would try to persuade a woman to get into bed by threatening that I would kiss her if she did not."

She laughed. Although she suspected both his distress at speaking of his brother and the longing she had tasted on his lips were both honest, she knew that tonight she owed him yet another debt.

She hoped she would be able to repay him . . . somehow.

Seven

Phoebe hid her yawn behind her hand as she stepped down off the bottom step at the front of the inn. She should not complain about not being able to sleep when Galen had spent the night on that uncomfortable chair. Yet finding any escape in her dreams had been impossible. She had tossed and turned, one moment too hot, the next too cold, as she battled with her own thoughts.

She should not have welcomed Galen's bold kiss. It had thrilled her in ways she could find no words to describe. That enchantment had not ended when he lifted his lips from hers. It had remained to sizzle through her like summer rain on a hot stone.

When she saw Galen speaking with a young man she did not know, she knew she should refrain from being tempted to admire how well Galen's coat accented the shoulders her fingers had only begun to explore. She should think of the tapestry of lies Galen had created rather than how expressive his face was. She might be able to hide her thoughts from Galen and this young man, but she could not hide from them herself.

Galen turned and smiled at her. She longed to rush to him and have him gather her into his arms again.

What an air-dreamer she was! Not only could she ruin everything she had spent the last five years doing, but she could destroy it for the future as well.

"There you are," Galen said with a chuckle. "I was wondering when you were going to turn out." Taking her hand, he drew her forward as he said, "Lady Phoebe, this is Tate, who will be driving us today."

"Where is Alfred?" she asked, nodding to the dark-haired coachee who looked too young to be in the box. Freckles dotted his cheeks and nose.

"On his way back to London." He steered her toward the carriage. "Tate has come from Townsend Hall to take us the rest of the way on our journey."

"From Townsend Hall? You sent a message there?"

His smile became wry. "Not directly. I had a lad take a note to Thistlewood Cottage, hoping that there was a carriage there we could use since mine could barely limp along the road. However, there was no carriage there, so the message was forwarded to Townsend Hall."

"But if someone were to follow the message . . ."

"Even on the unlikely chance that it was followed, it is well known that Sir Ledwin, who owns Thistlewood Cottage, and I are friends. It would not be unusual for a messenger to go from his house to mine." He chuckled as he added in a conspiratorial whisper, "And that very fact may confuse our pursuers."

She looked over her shoulder, unable to halt herself. "Mayhap we have confused them already, for I have seen no sign of anyone coming after us."

"So you believe that they have given up?"

"No." She let her breath slide out in a sigh. "I do not think they will give up. Ever."

* * *

Jerking away, Phoebe swallowed her cry of alarm as a hand touched her arm. She crouched back against the carriage wall. If one of the horrible men had exploded from her dreams into reality . . .

"Phoebe, we are at our destination," Galen said quietly.

"Thistlewood Cottage?"

His smile faded. "We should reach there tomorrow night. We are in Ledge-under-Water."

"Ledge-under-Water?" She giggled. In disbelief, she put her hand over her mouth. She had not been giddy like this since she was a child.

"You are tired, aren't you?" He cupped her elbow as he helped her out of the carriage to yet another yard in front of a simple whitewashed inn. "You should have slept later this morning."

"Or more last night."

"You didn't sleep?"

Dash it! She had not meant to reveal that. Her fatigue was making her mouth too loose. "I had two nights' sleep to catch up on."

"You should have taken advantage of the opportunity to fall asleep in the carriage sooner."

"I was not . . ." Words refused to form as they should in her brain.

His smile returned, the lazy, sensual smile that created a tingle along her as if he were caressing her. "You were not about to fall asleep in case you found yourself waking up in my arms."

"You are a bit too sure of your own charms, Galen."

"And you are a bit too unsure of your own charms." He put his hand over his stomach as it growled. "I believe that is the call for dinner."

"Galen." She glanced around the yard that was shadowed by two huge trees. "We are close to Bath.

It would be unseemly for us to share a room—even chastely—here."

"We have had no choice at the previous inns. However, I will ask here." He looked toward the stable, which was empty. "It looks as if the inn will not be crowded."

"Thank you."

"I would say it is my pleasure, but my pleasure would be to have you join me in the same room."

"So you might sleep in a hard chair?"

He laughed. "You are a callous woman, Ph—. Ah, I think it would be best if I did not speak your name here. You are right. We are quite close to Bath." He tapped his cheek, then smiled. "I have a cousin whose name is Jane."

"Do we really need such a charade?"

"It is said that 'tis better to be safe than sorry."

"Very well." She was hungry and tired, so she would go along with his attempt to protect her.

"Jane." He tapped his chin and grinned. "Jane Tate."

"You are naming me after your coachman?"

"Why not?"

That was an answer Phoebe did not have. She walked with Galen to the front door, which was wide open. The aromas of fresh bread and roasted meat greeted her, and she hoped her stomach would not grumble, too.

A smiling man walked across the neat stone floor. "Good evening."

"Good evening. I am Galen Townsend, and I would like rooms for myself and my companion."

The innkeeper regarded her with astonishment. She looked back at him without comment. She was no convenient, but she would play the part if it kept their pursuers from finding them.

"Of course," the innkeeper said. "I have a room . . ."

"Two rooms." Galen smiled at her. "If you have them, we need two rooms close to each other. As well, we will need suppers for both of us and my coachman in the stable, and we would appreciate something to break our fast on the morrow."

"As you wish, sir and miss . . ."

"Miss Jane Tate," she said, recalling the name Galen had selected for her.

"Welcome, Miss Tate. We are serving supper in the public room. However, I have a small room that may be more suited for a young lady. If you wish to eat now, I shall have fires laid in your rooms, so that any lingering chill will be gone."

"You are very kind," Galen said.

Phoebe thought she saw the flash of silver between the two men's hands, but she said nothing as she followed the innkeeper around the corner into a pleasant room. The windows were decorated with curtains of unbleached linen, and the tables were so well polished that the candles seemed to be burning on both ends. When Galen pulled out a chair for her, she sat gratefully.

Fresh bread and a bowl of soup were set in front of her. As Galen sat beside her, she picked up a spoon and took a bite. She smiled. The food was excellent.

"You look very happy, Miss Tate," Galen said with a chuckle.

"You should not call me that."

"Would you prefer I call you Jane?"

"I would prefer you eat your supper and appreciate this good food after the swill we have endured."

"Are you always this testy when you are tired?"

"Most likely." She had to smile in spite of herself. "How far are we from Bath?"

"If the clouds over the western hills do not bring

rain, we should be able to reach Bath sometime tomorrow." He smiled at a serving lass who put a trencher with roast beef and more bread next to his soup bowl.

"Thank heavens."

"And then what?" he asked, abruptly serious.

She put down her spoon. "I don't know."

"Do you have someone who will take you in until the chase winds down?"

"No."

"None of the families you have helped would play host to you?"

She stared down at the bowl, no longer hungry. "They are mostly poor, and adding another mouth around their table would be a huge burden."

"Good evening," called a jovial voice from the doorway.

Phoebe turned to see a middle-aged man whose girth vied with his height. His hair was graying, and his face was lined from years of being out in the sun. His well-made clothes suggested he was of the local gentry.

"Good evening," Galen said, coming to his feet. "Would you care to join us?"

"Thank you." He bowed his head toward Phoebe. "I am Rodney Dorrance, mayor of Ledge-under-Water."

"I am Townsend," Galen replied. "This is Miss Tate."

"Miss Tate." The pudgy man gave her a warm smile. "I hope you do not mind the intrusion."

"Of course not," she answered with what was only habit. She did not want to do anything but go to her room and sleep until she no longer ached with fatigue.

Mr. Dorrance sat across from her and held out his hand to the maid who brought him a tankard of ale.

"I have already dined, but I had hoped you would have news from beyond Ledge-under-Water."

"I am afraid we have nothing of excitement to share." Galen smiled and held up his mug for more ale. "There are no scandals in the government at the moment, and I have heard of nothing other than the usual pickpockets and burglars creating interest throughout London."

"You jest."

Phoebe asked, "Why do you say that, Mr. Dorrance?"

"The travelers who stayed here last night spoke of an uproar in London about Lady Midnight."

"Lady Midnight?" Galen asked. "Is this a new play?"

Mr. Dorrance rested both elbows on the table. "Far from that, Mr. Townsend, although discussion of Lady Midnight is as intriguing as a fine new drama."

"Then what is it?" asked Phoebe.

"Not an it, Miss Tate, but a she. Lady Midnight is rumored to be stealing convicts from ships and forcing them into the navy."

Phoebe glanced at Galen and hastily away. Lady Midnight? This tale might be based on her attempts to save some of the convicts being transported to the other side of the earth. If so, someone mistakenly believed this woman was helping the navy to obtain crews for the ships that controlled the seas from France to the Americas.

When Galen laughed, Phoebe flinched. He put his hand over hers as he said, "Ah, yes, I had heard something about such a woman, but no one seems to know much about her." He gave Mr. Dorrance a friendly grin. "Pray do not ask my Jane about this woman. Those who have spoken of this Lady Midnight to me would not be likely to be found in her company."

"Forgive me, Miss Tate," Mr. Dorrance hurried to say. "I did not realize that this was a subject unfit for a young lady's ears."

Rising, Phoebe said, "I shall leave you gentleman to your poker-talk."

Both men came to the feet as well. Telling Mr. Dorrance that he would return as soon as he escorted her to her room, Galen took her arm and walked with her toward the stairs to the upper floor.

"Your ankle must be better," he said.

"Yes."

"Can you climb the stairs?"

"Yes."

He gave her a sideways glance, but she said nothing else. As he followed her up the stairs, he remained as silent. He paused at the top next to a door. Taking her hand, he pressed a key into her hand.

"For your room," he said.

"Thank you."

He ran his hand along her cheek. "I know Mr. Dorrance's questions disturbed you greatly."

"I had no idea there were such rumors about."

"Now you are forewarned. These rumors may not have anything to do with . . ." He gave her a weary smile. "Do not worry, Phoebe. Soon there will be another tale to titillate the *ton* and this Lady Midnight will be forgotten."

"I hope you are right." She reached for her door, then paused. "At what hour do you wish to leave in the morning?"

"I will have a knock put on your door when we are ready to go."

"Thank you." She abruptly took his hands in hers. "Not just for tomorrow morning, Galen, but for all of this."

"It was no less than I could do."

"You should take care before you say that so swiftly. That is why I have been doing what I have."

"And what you intend to do again?"

"You know I cannot turn my back on those who need me."

He grasped her shoulders, shocking her, for he had been the epitome of gallantry this evening. "And you know, as well, that there will be those waiting for you to begin anew."

"But you said the rumors—"

"I do not speak of those engaged in idle talk, but of those who are much closer to the truth."

"*They* are never far from my mind."

When he bid her a good evening, Phoebe thought for a moment he would kiss her as he had last night. Instead, he turned on his heel and went to the stairs. Her first reaction was hurt that he had not at least tried. When he glanced back at her, she could not mistake the craving in his eyes, for not even the dim light could hide it.

She took a single step toward him. She froze when that enticing smile tilted his lips. Was she out of her mind? Going back to the door, she opened it. Hastily she shut it behind her before the teasings of her heart sent her rushing back to him.

The candles must have gutted themselves, for the only light was dim starglow flowing through the lone window. She was surprised. The innkeeper had appeared to be so competent and concerned about his guests. She groped through the unfamiliar shadows, hoping to find the bed before she bumped into it.

She hit a table. Setting her bonnet on it, she waited for her eyes to adjust to the darkness. She loosened her bracelet. It clattered on the bare wood as she put it next to her bonnet.

Even the fire on the hearth was out. Odd. She had

been certain the innkeeper had vowed to have the fires lit while they ate. She took a deep breath and gagged on the odor of wet ashes. Someone had doused the fire. Her steps faltered. What was all this about?

Hands reached out of the blackness to grasp Phoebe. She tried to scream, but a sweaty palm over her mouth stifled it. Her captor pulled her back against a sturdy male chest. Light from a lantern flared in her eyes. She was blinded and could not determine how many people were in the room. The light vanished again before she could do more than blink.

"Silence, woman. You will be sorry if someone heard you." The fingers holding Phoebe dug into her painfully, and she groaned against the hand.

When the hand at her mouth loosened, she drew in her breath to scream, but a gag was tied around her head. Her hair was twisted into the knot. She heard a cruel laugh, then she was pushed backward onto a bed. In terror, she fought for her balance and stared at the dark figure leaning over her.

She swung her fist at him. Curses filled the room. She kicked him, and he groaned. She tried to escape, but he pushed her back on the hard mattress and rolled her up into the heavy quilt.

She was picked up and thrown carelessly over his shoulder. She moaned. Screaming was futile. She must save her strength to escape. She tried to gauge where they were going, but the quilt covered her face.

Panic lashed her. She kicked at him again and struck flesh. He grunted in pain, then pressed her legs against his chest. Her head grew light from hanging upside down over his shoulder. She could breathe only the heavy air seeping through the quilt. Her nose bounced against his back, and tears streamed down her cheeks.

The stairs he was descending could not be the ones

at the entrance of the inn. Someone would have seen them. But would anyone notice a man carrying a quilt? She tried to wiggle, hoping to catch any eye that might be aimed in their direction. The gag muted her moan as she was bounced on his sharp shoulder bones.

Low voices and the whinny of a horse reached her ears. She was dropped onto a flat surface, which lurched into motion. When she started to roll out of the quilt, hands held her to the wagon bed.

Galen! The scream could be heard only in her head. She shuddered against the thick blanket. So many questions fled through her head. Someone must have seen her and recognized her. Had all the talk about Lady Midnight been only a ruse to keep them so upset that they would not notice someone from London sneaking into the inn?

Galen! He might be kept speaking with Mr. Dorrance for so long that he would never been able to trace her. And what if he could? He might be walking right into trouble that even he could not get them out of. Sweet heavens, if he followed, he might be hurt.

She fought against the quilt, but she could not loosen it. The man's hand must be pressed over where the quilt should have come open. She ran her feet across the boards of the wagon, looking for a crevice between them. If she could slip her toe into one, she might be able to pull herself back out of this smothering cocoon. She stretched out her foot. It was slapped hard.

Abruptly the wagon stopped. Heavy hands gripped her. She silenced her moan as she was set over the wide shoulder again. She kicked both feet at her captor. He swore and clamped his arms around her knees, pinning them once more against his chest.

Phoebe was carried a short distance. The clump of boots against the earth became a hollow sound. They must have entered a building with a wooden floor. Suddenly she was dumped on the floor. Her gasp of pain was muted behind the gag. No one touched her, so she wondered if she had been left alone. She would not wait to discover. She must escape.

Pushing against the swaddling of the quilt, she unwrapped herself and reached up to remove the dirty handkerchief around her head. Angrily, she flung the soaked material away.

A board creaked not far from her. Looking up, she discovered a huge man leaning on a half wall and regarding her in silence. Her brows lowered as she stared back at the man. He was massive. From where she sat, it seemed his head must brush the rafters of the barn. His hair was as black as his glower. Thin lips turned up in a smile as his serpentine tongue slowly licked them. The leer on his florid face and the strength of his muscular body, which threatened the seams of his shirt, added to her fear.

Who was he? She had never seen him on the docks down along the Thames.

When he spoke, his voice was immense, too. "Jane Tate?"

Phoebe hesitated. *Jane Tate?* Who . . . ? The name that Galen had given her to protect her. What did that name have to do with all of this?

"Answer me. Are you Jane Tate?"

If she said no, she might have to own to her real name. This could be a way for her pursuers to get her to betray herself, although why they would resort to this was something she could not imagine. But if she said yes, what might this man do to her? She must learn more about what this was all about.

"Why do you want to know that? Who are you?" She stood slowly, for her whole body ached. Pushing back her tangled hair, she demanded, "Why have you abducted me?"

The man straightened to his full height, well over six feet. His shirt was crisscrossed with grime matching the filthy blacksmithing tools scattered around the barn. Her eyes widened when she discovered she was standing in a stall.

"I can see why you twisted his head," the man murmured as his gaze fondled her from head to foot.

Phoebe folded her arms in front of her, longing to block his eager gaze which seemed to cut through her gown. "I do not know what you are talking about."

His tongue slithered along his lips. "No? You do not know how you persuaded Jimmy to turn away from his wife and family before leaving him so heartbroken that he hanged himself?"

"What?" She stared at him. Was he insane? No, he was furious, but it was a deeply seething fury that had nothing to do with madness. "I don't know what you are speaking of."

"You don't, Jane Tate?"

"But I am not Jane Tate." She could not dissemble any longer. Not when he wore that livid expression.

His eyes narrowed. "I heard what your new lover called you. Jane Tate." He grasped her arm, jerking her closer. "And you did not deny it was your name when I asked you before. Why are you denying it now?"

"Because Jane Tate is not my name."

"Your lies are worthless." He laughed with the same cruelty he had displayed at the inn.

She pulled away from him. Desperately she looked for a way to escape. Although her eyes had adjusted to the dim interior of the smithy, she could not see the door.

"You caused my brother's death," he growled. "I think 'tis time you paid the debt you owe us."

"I owe you nothing! I am not the woman you are seeking." Hay pricked through her stockings as she backed away from him. When he seized her arms, she screamed, "Let me go!"

"No, Miss Tate. Tonight you will pay for my brother's murder."

"Murder?" She searched his contorted face. "But you said he hanged himself!"

He shook her so viciously she feared her brain would rattle loose. Through the rumble in her ears, she heard him snarl, "He was murdered! By you and your cold heart."

She gasped with astonishment. He *was* deranged! She was alone in this smithy with a madman. Somehow she had to make him realize that he had made a horrible mistake. Her voice trembled as she said, "Sir, you must let me explain. It is not as you think."

His fingers twisted in her hair until she cried out. He tilted her head back and leered down at her. "It is *exactly* as I think. I want you to suffer as we have, pretty Jane. Pretty, pretty Jane. I must own that I had planned on killing you at the inn . . . until I saw you." He smiled as he ran a broad hand along her waist. He tugged her against his bulky body. "You are so willing to share yourself with your new lover. Let me see what drove my brother from his family and to his death."

"No!" she screamed before his mouth clamped over hers.

She tried to shove his hands away. Her cries of protest resounded deep in his throat as he reached to unclasp the row of buttons along the back of her dress. Her gown gaped. His mouth moved in a slimy caress along her neck as he slipped her sleeve down her arm. She screamed again.

She must stop him. Stop him from killing her and stop him from *this!* Too many depended on her. She could not let them suffer because her life ended by error in this filthy smithy.

He pushed her backward toward the pile of hay. She fell, and her dress tore. She moaned as she struck the floor. When she looked up to see his eyes bulging with the yearning for vengeance, she shrieked and tried to roll to her feet. He dropped to his knees and pinned her to the filthy floor. She tried to push him away, but he laughed as his mouth descended onto the skin visible above her dress's drooping neckline. His knee pushed her legs apart, and she screamed in pure terror as he reached to unbutton his breeches. Closing her eyes, she tensed. There was no escape from this nightmare.

Suddenly the heavy weight over her vanished. She heard a deep voice say, "That is no way to treat a lady, my friend."

She opened her eyes to see Galen shove the man away from her. The man ripped a knife from the wall behind him and swung it. Galen jumped back, nearly stumbling over her. She pushed herself to her feet and groaned when her dress threatened to fall off. Pulling it up, she cried out in horror as the man aimed the knife at Galen again. This time, Galen reeled back and dropped to one knee. The big man rushed toward him, the knife raised.

She ran to halt him. He brushed her back as if she had no more strength than a moth. She struck the floor again. Her head whirled with pain. Hearing a grunt, she forced her eyes to focus and saw Galen easily drop her abductor with a single well placed blow to the man's face. The knife vanished in the darkness.

Phoebe stared in disbelief as Galen pulled a pocket

pistol from beneath his coat. Where had he gotten that? She could not ask as he pointed it at the man.

"Get out of here," Galen ordered, his voice brittle.

The man stood and lurched away, holding his hand over his bloody nose.

Galen knelt by where she huddled on the floor. "Phoebe, are you all right?" Gently, he smoothed her skirt back down her legs.

She nodded, but did not move.

"Then sit up. He is gone."

"I can't!" she whispered. Embarrassment created heat around her face. "My dress is completely undone. When I stood a moment ago, it nearly fell to the floor."

"I noticed."

"You did not! You were busy with *that beast!*"

"Not too busy to notice the pink ribbons in the top of your shift." He laughed as he put the gun back under his coat. "If that is the only problem, Phoebe, I can remedy that. I shall hook you up. Turn around. I promise you I will be a perfect gentleman."

She sat and stared at the wall as he competently redid the many small buttons. It was not easy to ignore his gentle touch or his breath, which was enticingly warm against her neck. "Thank you," she murmured, not wanting to speak more loudly. Then she might not be able to stop from blurting that she wished there had been even more buttons, so his fascinating touch would not be coming to an end so quickly.

He held out his hand to aid her to her feet and asked, "Are you all right?"

"Yes." It was a lie. Her knees wobbled, and her head swam alarmingly. As she started to step out of the stall, she stumbled. He caught her elbow and drew her closer to the undeniable strength of his firm body. She stiffened.

"Come now, Phoebe. Didn't I just rescue you?" His voice was uneven. "Have some faith in me!"

She tried to move away, but her legs sagged beneath her. She leaned against the door of the stall. "I don't know why I should trust you when you were the one who got me into all this."

"Me?"

"Yes, you and your plan to give me an alias. The alias you chose was the name of the very woman who ruined that man's brother's life. Please release me."

"I don't think that would be a good idea." His voice had become oddly breathless. Or was it just that her ears were so filled with the echo of her rapid heartbeat that she could not hear him well?

"At this moment, I care little what you think!" she retorted. She should not be thinking of how enticing his fingers were, but how furious she was at him for getting her into this predicament.

"You have made that very clear."

"I was abducted," she said as they walked out of the stall.

"True."

"I could have been killed."

"True." His retort was terse.

"I could have been—I could have been—" She shivered and hid her face in her hands.

Taking her hands, he drew them down. His face was strained, but he struggled to smile. "I know you blame me, Phoebe, but I devised the plan only to protect you."

"True." She smiled, then laced her fingers through his. "Forgive me, Galen. I know you were trying to help. I appreciate you being so heroic tonight."

He offered her a wry smile. "Playing the dashing hero tonight was not my intention. Let's continue this conversation somewhere else." He tilted toward her. "I am sorry that I put you in such danger."

A tremor swept through her as his words rustled close to her ear. "Nothing has gone as it should since I last left my house. Every good intention has dissolved into disaster."

"It would be a disaster if your pursuers had found you."

"How did you find me?"

"Tate saw your friend come out of the inn and was suspicious when he noted that the rolled blanket on the man's shoulder moved as if it were alive. He alerted me. We followed."

Phoebe tightened her arms around Galen's arm as he led her cautiously through the cluttered building. His foot hit something. At its metallic clang, he cursed. When she laughed at his original turn of phrase, he grinned but weakly.

They emerged into the night. A shadowy, amorphous object became, as they neared it, a carriage. His smile grew even more brittle as he opened the door. A thousand questions battered at her lips, but she said nothing as Galen took her fingers to hand her in.

"Tate," he ordered, "take us to . . ." His voice became a groan. He shivered, then collapsed to the ground, his fingers pressed to his side.

She knelt beside him. When he moaned, she put her hand over his hand. She gasped when she saw blood on her fingers. Carefully she peeled his hand away. His waistcoat was blotched near his left side. The man's knife must have struck him. Why hadn't he told her?

"Tate!" she called.

The lad ran from the front of the carriage to where Galen was lying. He swore, not bothering to curb his tongue. She did not chide him.

"Shall I put him in the carriage, my lady?"

"Yes." She faltered, then asked, "Can you?"

Tate nodded. When he lifted Galen from the ground, flinging Galen's arm over his shoulder, Phoebe put one hand against Tate's back and the other on Galen's to steady both of them. She bit her lip to say nothing as Tate fought for each step to the carriage. Somehow, the lad hefted Galen inside.

"Thank you," Phoebe said. "Thank goodness you are stronger than you appear."

"A coachee needs to make sure his passengers get home, no matter what condition they are in," he said with a proud smile. It wavered as he stared at Galen. "Will he be all right?"

"Yes," she replied, wishing she had the confidence that was in her voice.

"Where do you wish us to go?"

"To Thistlewood Cottage."

"Can Lord Townsend travel that far?"

"I hope so." Her voice broke. "I hope so, because he must."

Eight

Could it be possible? Galen wondered if he had again climbed out of the nursery window on the uppermost floor of Townsend Hall and slid down the huge tree, unable to halt himself. Then he had jarred every rib and left his skin raw. He had been a hero among his friends when he returned to school to show off his injuries, and he had never let any of them know how much he hurt.

As much as he did now.

He touched his side and winced. Through his covers, thick bandages were wrapped around him, the heaviest part directly over the convergence of the pain that ached through every breath.

"Take care," came a soft voice.

Phoebe's voice!

Was she hurt, too? No, that made no sense. She would not be so close if she was injured. Or would she be? He could not form a single rational thought.

Just pain.

A cool cloth dabbed at his brow, and Galen relaxed back into the soft mattress. Straining, he turned his head to see a slender arm right in front of his eyes. He followed the arm to even more pleasurable curves. It took more effort than he would have guessed to raise his gaze past them to a determined chin and exquisite lips. He groaned and closed his eyes before his gaze could meet hers.

"Take care," Phoebe whispered again, and he was startled to hear what sounded like amusement in her voice.

"I am glad you find something humorous in all of this."

"What?" Her astonishment sounded sincere. She continued to brush the damp cloth against his forehead as she said, "I can assure you, Galen, that I do not derive any diversion from anything that happened last night."

"Last night?" He sounded like a blasted echo, repeating everything she said, but his own thoughts remained too scattered for him to trust them. "Where are we?"

Phoebe walked away from the bed, and he was tempted to shout after her. Just the very idea of raising his voice sent another throb of pain through him. He forced his eyes to remain open and looked to see where she had vanished to.

He was in a small bedchamber. The furniture was simple, but fitting for a room with stone walls and floors. Open rafters above had no sign of dust or birds, and he could see the crisscross pattern of the boards that supported the roof. A pair of windows, one in the wall on either side of the bed, were hidden behind thick drapes. Even so, a hint of starlight peered through, and he knew it must be approaching midnight.

At the clatter of glass, he turned his head the other way to see Phoebe had crossed the room to a table where a tray was waiting. She was pouring something into a glass, which she carried back to where he was lying.

"This is Thistlewood Cottage," she said, handing him the glass.

Galen took a careful sip. Wine. It was just what he needed to rid himself of the disgusting flavor left in his mouth by . . . By what? He could not recall what had happened before he woke up here.

"Are you hungry?" she asked.

He lifted his gaze from the wine to her. By Jove, he had let himself forget how beautiful she was. He had been concentrating so much on keeping her out of harm's way that he had closed his eyes to how hers twinkled or how the color in her cheeks seemed to be brushed on by a mere zephyr.

"Should I be hungry?"

"You have not eaten since last night at the inn in Ledge-under-Water." She smiled. "The doctor gave you some powders in wine while he tended to stitching the wound in your side. You slept all the day."

He looked at his glass. "Does this glass have powders stirred into it?"

"Do you need something to ease your pain?"

"I would rather have the answers to some questions."

She nodded, and he noticed her hand trembled as she lifted her own glass to take a sip. He wanted to take her fingers and offer her some silent comfort. When he started to shift to reach for it, pain lashed him. He groaned out a question.

"Tate and I managed to get you back into the carriage," Phoebe replied, "and we drove here at top speed."

"I owe you an apology, I fear."

She waved aside his words. "You did nothing wrong. All your actions, even your unfortunate choice of a name for me, were aimed at protecting me. For that, I cannot fault you."

"If I had had any idea that Miss Jane Tate was such a lusty wench, creating all sorts of trouble, I believe I would have selected another name." He took another sip of the pungent wine. Its heat seemed to add strength to his wobbly limbs.

"I believe you would have." She laughed and sat on the chair by the bed. Her expression grew somber. "However, I must assume that the hullabaloo you created at the inn when you and Tate raced off to my rescue gained much attention."

"Yes, I am afraid so. To own the truth, Phoebe, I was not thinking of protecting your secret when I feared for your very life."

She patted his hand. "I know."

His fingers captured hers, not letting her draw them away. "You should know that if that cur had hurt you, I would have seen him dead."

"That would have created even more of an unforgettable scene."

Galen stared at her in disbelief, for he had not expected her to respond with a hint of humor in her voice. "By Jove, Phoebe, you make it difficult for a man to play your hero."

"I do not want a hero." Coming to her feet, she pulled her hand out of his. "I want to return to the work that I have pledged to do. I want to know if my household is unharmed. I want to learn if Jasper was able to escape from those chasing us."

"Your household is unsettled, but fine. Your man is recovering at your country house."

Phoebe whirled to face Galen. "How do you know this?"

"Alfred gave me the note you had written to your household."

"But he promised it would be delivered."

"I delivered it. To the flames, so it would not betray you."

"You should not have done that. I needed to warn my household—"

"They were warned. I told Alfred to make inquiries as soon as he reached London, but to leave no sign of why," he said quietly. "He sent word to me, which arrived at the inn last night just after you retired."

"And you did not tell me?"

"When would I have had time? When I was teaching your erstwhile admirer a lesson in good manners?"

She rubbed her hands together uneasily. "I am sorry. This has been so distressing."

He frowned. As his gaze settled on her soft lips, he saw two crystalline tears glistening at the corners of her eyes. Berating himself for thinking of her inviting mouth when she had been treated so cruelly, he could not keep from imagining the pleasure to be found in arousing the desires she kept so tightly restrained. He imagined as well that doing so would reward him with a slapped face.

"I did not want to have you fly off into a pelter when you learned that your message had not been delivered."

"Flying off into a pelter is not something that I do." She grasped the back of the chair, and he noticed she was not wearing the silver bracelet she had worn since she had entered his carriage near the Pool. "By all that's blue, Galen, I have been able to rescue nearly tenscore people from being banished from England, but you think me incapable of common sense."

"Common sense? I believe you have an abundance of that, but, Phoebe, for someone who is defying the law and has been labeled a traitor, you have too much trust. If anyone—anyone at all—had chanced to find a note from you in your house on Grosvenor Square, then this sojourn to Thistlewood Cottage would have been for naught."

"As long as they are forewarned, I guess you have done no damage."

"It was not my intention to cause me damage in your eyes. I had wanted only to help." He took her left hand. "Where is your bracelet, Phoebe?"

"It was left behind, along with my bonnet, at the inn."

"I can send a messenger to—"

"No need. I doubt if it is still there." She rubbed her hands together. "If I had known that you had sent a message to my house, I would not have made the arrangements I did for tomorrow night."

"Tomorrow night?" He pushed himself up to sit, then feared he would be sick in front of her. He pressed his hand to his stomach and groaned again. If there was any spot where he did not hurt, he had not found it yet.

"Yes. Vogel told me—"

"Vogel?"

"The butler here."

"There is a butler here?" He frowned as he looked around the simple room again as she walked to the door and back. "I thought you said we were at Thistlewood Cottage. Where are we really?"

"We *are* at Thistlewood Cottage." She stopped pacing and faced him.

"Really?"

"Yes." She smiled. "Lying to my only ally would be foolish, especially when it is something of such insignificance."

"A butler does not fit with my image of a *cottage.*"

Putting her hand on the post at the foot of the bed, she laughed wearily. "Nothing about this place fits with *my* image of a cottage. We are on the edge of the city of Bath, not in some pastoral setting. This house must have been built when Good King Hal was a boy, and it has wings wandering in every direction as well as a full staff."

"A full staff?" He swore under his breath.

When color rose up her face, she turned away to go to one of the windows. She drew back the drapes, letting moonlight flow onto the floor.

"Forgive me," he said, "for speaking so."

"I have heard much worse."

"I am sure you have, but you should not expect to hear it from me." He sighed, then downed the rest of the wine in his glass. "It is not easy to be inconspicuous when we are staying at a grand house in Bath instead of the small cottage I had anticipated."

"I have often found that the best way to hide something is to keep it right in plain sight."

"That makes no sense. Are you sure you are not the one who got a facer?"

She laughed. "My head is quite thick, or so I have been told on numerous occasions. It can tolerate quite a bit." Again she grew serious as she added, "I hope yours can endure a lot as well, because we are having a gathering here tomorrow night."

"You must have taken more than a knock in your head. Tomorrow night?"

"Yes. Just a few friends who will be arriving to play cards and share some conversation." She raised her hands as he opened his mouth to retort. "Hear me out, Galen. As I said, it is often easiest to hide something in plain sight. If suspicion has chased us from London, we must counter it. No one with any common sense would host a gathering the day after traveling from London to Bath. They would rest up a bit first."

"Anyone with common sense would."

"So, my idea is that if we host a gathering tomorrow night, we can speak of how we have relaxed in the gardens here while we recovered from our trip from London."

He continued to frown. "That may be so, but what reason do you give for you and me traveling alone from Town to this so-called cottage?"

"Why, I was only doing as a lady should when I encountered you on the Bath road after your carriage broke down." She smiled. "As Alfred had to limp back to London in your carriage, it will give countenance to the whole story."

"You are devious," he said, his grin returning.

"Only if you think you can stand by my side tomorrow evening to welcome the guests I have invited."

Galen sagged back into the pillows as he tried to give no mind to the ache scoring his forehead. "How many?"

"About twenty." She refilled his glass. "You mentioned the names of some friends while we were riding here. I sent them invitations as well as an invitation to Mr. and Mrs. Lyttle, who are friends of mine."

"It seems you have this all set."

Putting the bottle of wine back on the table, she said, "Only if you think you can do this."

"How can I say no?"

"No is not difficult to say."

He took her hand and held it beneath his on the covers. When she would have drawn it back, he curled his fingers around hers. "It is difficult for *you* to say."

"I told that beast in the smithy no very easily."

"And you have told me no, as well." He stroked her soft skin. When she quivered at the chaste sensation, he thought of how delightfully she had trembled when he kissed her. A craving that eclipsed even the pain in his side surged through him. "But, my dear, you cannot say no to those you believe are in need."

"Not now."

He pulled her down to sit beside him on the bed. She cried out in dismay, but he kept her eyes even with his as he asked, "Does that mean you do not want to continue this work that endangers you?"

"Of course not."

"Odd, for it sounds as if you just did." Putting the glass on the chair by the bed, he met her gaze evenly.

"I have my obligations, Galen." Her chin rose as she offered him her coolest smile. It was wasted because he could see the pain in her eyes.

His other hand brushed her cheek, and he winced when he stretched the wound in his side. The cur's knife had only grazed him, but the pain suggested that the blade had sliced far into him. Swallowing that groan, he said, "Lady Midnight's obligations?"

All color vanished from her face. "Did Mr. Dorrance say anything more about those tales?"

"Not enough to tell me if they truly could be connected with you."

"You believe it is a coincidence?"

"I would *like* to believe that."

She sighed. "I don't believe that it is just a coincidence either. That is why I am asking you to risk your recovery with this gathering tomorrow evening."

"If you will make it a *conversazione*, it will be easier for me. I can sit and complain about the injury I received yesterday when my horse dumped me as I was trying to take a fence. That will explain my sore ribs, although I will endure ribbing at my inability to keep my seat."

"Good."

"You realize what a blow this will be to my pride as a horseman, don't you?"

"No." Phoebe faltered, then said, "I really know very little about you."

He regarded her with amazement. "That is true. We have not had much time for chitchat. I know little about you other than what *on dits* says and what takes you to the Pool."

"I can say much the same of you."

"Mayhap because there is little else to say."

She laughed. "Come now, Galen. Surely you are not unaware of what is said about the dashing Lord Townsend who sweeps young misses off their feet and endangers their reputations."

"I do not feel the least bit dashing at the moment."

"Are you in great pain?" she asked, her smile vanishing.

He put his hand over his side. "I have been better, but you need not fret about me because of this injury. To own the truth, I have hurt myself far worse through my own unthinking behavior." His eyes twinkled with the merriment that warned her that he was not exaggerating. "And 'tis far better to be wounded in the gallantry of protecting a fair lady from a blackguard than in trying to sneak out of the nursery and falling out of a tree when my nightshirt was caught on a limb."

Phoebe laughed. She could not halt herself. The image of the customarily elegant Galen Townsend hanging from a tree branch by his nightshirt was wildly amusing. Wiping tears from her eyes, she met his gaze. Her breath snagged in her throat as she saw the naughty child he had been mirrored in his sparkling eyes. He was a man who delighted in a challenge and believed he could do anything he set his mind on. Even rescuing her from her own misstep on the docks.

He did not speak nor did he touch her, but she leaned toward him, wanting to be so close to him that she could savor his breath on her face and hear his heartbeat, which was so much steadier than hers. Slowly her fingers rose to stroke his cheek that was a strange shade beneath his tan.

"I should not," she whispered, drawing back her hand.

"Because we are alone here on my bed?" he asked as softly.

"No, because I might hurt you worse."

"These fingers could not hurt me." He tilted his head and kissed her fingertips, one by one. His own hand brought her lips closer to his. "And a kiss would certainly make me feel better."

A knock came at the door. Phoebe jumped to her feet, nearly tripping over the chair. She gripped it to keep it from falling to the floor.

"I have never seen a guiltier face," Galen said with a chuckle.

Giving him an uneven smile, she went to the door. She opened it and let in a tall man.

She slipped out into the corridor as she heard Galen greet the man with "Roland, what in the blazes are *you* doing here?" A pause, then, "Phoebe, wait!"

Phoebe did not answer. Walking along the passage, she let her shoulders ease from their straight line. Roland had welcomed her on her arrival and introduced himself as "Lord Townsend's man." When Tate had brought the carriage from Townsend Hall, Roland had insisted on traveling to Thistlewood Cottage as well.

She would leave Galen's valet to serve him while she tried to regain her composure. She should not have been in Galen's room alone. Where was every iota of propriety that she once had taken such pride in? She was becoming as indifferent to the canons of Society as one of the high-skirts by the Pool.

Coming down the trio of steps to the next lower

level of the house, which went up and down along the hill overlooking the river that split Bath in half, she did not look back. The walls here were constructed of stone, but old tapestries and portraits that were nearly as ancient added a graciousness to the rooms with the deep-set windows and bare rafters. She walked through the room to the terrace beyond the open doors.

The city of Bath was set between the hills below. She rested her hands on the iron railing and admired it. She had not been to Bath since she was a young girl, although her friend Mrs. Lyttle had asked her to pay a call often in the past five years.

The curve of the Crescent and the maze of the streets were marked by lamplight that reflected back the starlight overhead. A gentle breeze sifted through the branches nearby. Hearing the rattle of a wagon, she sighed. These sights and sounds had been so familiar both on Grosvenor Square and, oddly, by the Pool when she had made her way there in the depths of the night.

Wrapping her arms around herself, she smiled up at the sky. She loved this time of year and this time of night. Everything was so alive and yet so quiet.

"You look happy."

She whirled. "Galen, what are you doing here? You should be resting."

Taking cautious steps out onto the terrace, he walked to the railing. "I wanted to assure myself that you were all right."

"Me? I was barely hurt." She pulled up a chair for him. Sitting on a stone bench facing him, she added, "Galen Townsend, you are want-witted to leave your bed."

"Mayhap, but I wish to be sure that you are fine. I was not sure if it was just Roland's arrival that might have found you in a most indelicate position with me, or if something else was bothering you." He held out his hand.

She took it and smiled. "I will be fine when I return to Town and what I should be doing."

"You are going to be troublesome, I fear."

"Troublesome?"

"I thought you understood that you must remain here until the furor is over." He paused, then added, "Even after I go back to London."

"When you go, I shall as well."

"No."

"But, Galen—"

"I will be returning to London the day after tomorrow."

Phoebe stood. "Are you out of your mind? You were stabbed. You need to heal."

"I was badly scratched. Nothing more." Pushing himself to his feet, he said, "I must go to London to fulfill my own obligations. When it is safe for you to return, I will send you a message to let you know."

"That is kind of you, but I cannot linger here."

"You must. If your pursuers do not find you soon, they are certain to give up."

She went back to the iron railing and stared down at the river. "They will not give up so easily."

"All the more reason for you to remain here." His voice came from close behind her. When his hands settled on her shoulders, he said, "You will be safe here while I do what I must."

"Rescue your brother from his own foolishness?"

"Yes."

"Do you think that is possible?" she asked, facing him.

He scowled. "I have to hope so."

Nine

"Excellent," Phoebe said as Vogel motioned for a maid to put the last tray of glasses on the table by the double doors leading to the terrace. Light flowed through the doors and over the rugs to merge with the sunshine coming through the trio of windows set into the opposite wall.

The butler nodded, his face as somber as if they were planning a funeral instead of an evening of cards and conversation. He adjusted one corner of the tablecloth, which was embroidered with a crest that must belong to Sir Ledwin's family because she had seen it repeated throughout the cottage.

As he walked out of the room, Phoebe looked around her. How odd it was to be planning a gathering in a house that was not her own! She was accustomed to the expansive height of the ballroom in Brackenton Park and the elegance of the house on Grosvenor Square.

Tapping her finger against her chin, she tried to remember the last time she had entertained at either place. She sat on a wooden bench by the windows. The last time had been the night before she heard that Jasper's younger brother had been sentenced to seven years' transportation to the far side of the world. She had been the hostess at an evening *conversazione* much like the one she had planned for tonight.

"Lady Phoebe?"

She looked toward the door to the hall. A young footman stood there. Although he tried to copy Vogel's stern expression, his lips twitched. She was not sure whether he was struggling not to laugh or it was something else altogether.

"Yes?" she asked.

Squaring his shoulders, he said, "Mr. Townsend, my lady."

Phoebe heard herself ask the footman to bring Galen's brother in, but the footman had no time to convey the message before a tall, strikingly handsome man with dark ruddy hair strode into the room. The resemblance between the brothers was strong from their height to the well-tailored clothes that bespoke of their place among the *ton*.

"Welcome, Mr. Townsend," she said, finding her voice as he stared at her with the same appraising look he was giving the room. What was Galen's brother doing here? Mayhap it was as simple as Carr had run out of funds for his bachelor's fare in Town, and he was coming here to depend on his brother's boundless generosity.

Dash it! This would mean that Galen would not be leaving on the morrow for London. Her heart leaped with joy even as she reminded herself that she would find it more difficult to go back to Town if Galen remained here. She wanted to stay with him to discover more about the sensations that swept over her each time he touched her. But she was needed in London. She must go back.

Carr Townsend pulled off his gloves and tossed them into his hat. Handing both to the footman, he said, "I had understood my brother could be found here. Who are you?"

"Phoebe Brackenton."

Mr. Townsend's air of disdain vanished as a calculating glint came into his eyes. Did he think she would not notice as he bent over her hand? Mayhap he was so assured of his charm that he considered it a matter beneath his concern.

"My lady, forgive me for not recognizing you."

"I do not believe we have been introduced previously, although we have spoken at least once in London."

He leaned one shoulder against the open doorway. "That is true. I would be a vulgar cad if I failed to see such a lovely addition at so many of the gatherings we both have attended during the beginning of this Season."

"Excuse me while I make certain your brother is aware that you are calling."

He stepped in front of her. "As soon as I walked into the house, a footman scurried away to do exactly that. Another brought me here, apparently believing that you should know of my arrival. You do not need to rush away, too."

"Of course not." Phoebe kept her fingers from curling into fists at her side. She should not judge Mr. Townsend before she knew him. *On dits* had labeled Galen a rake of the first order, but he had been a gentleman with her. "Will you sit down, Mr. Townsend?"

"I would rather you offer me something to take the dust of the road from my throat." He walked past her to the table and picked up a glass. "Is there any brandy in this house?"

Going to a bellpull, Phoebe tugged on it. Vogel appeared in the door and nodded at her request to bring some brandy.

"I trust," Mr. Townsend said as he motioned for her to sit, "that you will entertain me with an explanation of what you are doing with my brother at Sir Ledwin Woods's house."

She sat and folded her hands in her lap. "Your brother was kind enough to act as my host after I encountered him when his carriage broke down. He—"

"Carr!" Galen's glad shout echoed off the ceiling.

Phoebe came to her feet, wanting to warn Galen to take care that he did not hurt himself again as he went to greet his brother. She said nothing as Galen slapped his brother companionably on the back. Mr. Townsend chuckled and went to where a maid was bringing a tray with two bottles on it.

Grasping the brandy, Mr. Townsend poured enough to fill two glasses. He handed one to Galen before taking a deep drink of his.

"Ah," Mr. Townsend said. "That is just what I needed after that long trip." He turned to smile at Phoebe. "I have had the opportunity to meet your companion, and I suspect you have found just what you need, too."

She stiffened. Mayhap gossip had been mistaken when they labeled Galen Townsend as a prime rake. Clearly his brother had left his manners behind him in Town.

"Yes, I have," Galen replied. He smiled at her. When she did not return it, his expression wavered. He filled a glass with wine and held it out to her. "Phoebe has been kind enough to agree to hostess a rout for me this evening. I assume you will join us."

Mr. Townsend's nose wrinkled. "Bath society is bound to bring on a bout of ennui."

"So why are you here?" Phoebe asked, then sipped her wine as she watched Mr. Townsend's eyes narrow.

"I discovered Galen was gone from Town, so I thought I would find out where he had taken himself. Imagine my surprise to discover Alfred despairing about the damage to your carriage, brother. He did reassure me that you had not been hurt in an upset, but I thought I would see for myself."

Phoebe looked away, hoping her face was not ablaze with her embarrassment. Carr Townsend might have a sullied reputation and a vexing attitude, but he had traveled nearly the breadth of England to be certain that his brother was unscathed by whatever had damaged the carriage. Mayhap she had misjudged him.

When she excused herself, leaving the brothers to talk, she reminded herself that Mr. Townsend's arrival should be good tidings for her. Galen would not be leaving.

Only she would be . . . as soon as she knew it was safe to go to London.

Phoebe hurried into her bedchamber. Where had the day gone? She had spent the afternoon in the garden, tending to some of the flowers that seemed in need of attention, and because she wanted to avoid Carr Townsend's attentions. After he had monopolized the conversation at luncheon, refusing to heed any opinions but his own, she had decided he was the most irritating man she had ever met. He could not be accused of any misdeed, for his words were always sugary-sweet. Yet the undertone of some stronger emotion was always there. She did not want to explore closely enough to discover if he was jealous of his brother or if he simply understood that he could be as ill man-

He gave the order to his coachman, then sat back, folding his arms over his chest. "Tell me why you were fleeing these men, Phoebe."

It did not take long for her to explain how, when she had learned that Jasper's younger brother was about to be sent to Australia, she had devised this scheme to bribe underpaid sailors to release some of the prisoners to her. By the time she was explaining how easily she found work for the prisoners in Exmoor and how they must stay there for the length of their sentence before they could return home, the carriage was turning into the street leading to Grosvenor Square.

"You are mad, you know," Galen said when she finished telling how everything had gone off course tonight.

"Mayhap, but it is something I feel I must do."

As the carriage started to slow, Galen glanced out the window. With a curse, he threw the hatch open again. "Alfred, keep driving."

"Where to, my lord?"

"Take the Bath road."

"My lord?"

"You heard me."

"Aye, my lord." He shut the hatch.

"The Bath road?" Phoebe repeated, sure she had misheard him. "But my home is right over—"

Galen pulled her away from the window. "Let me guess. It's the one where our friend's carriage is slowing in front of even now."

"Our friend?" Her eyes widened as she saw the coach that held the man and the two sailors. "I must warn my household."

"How can you do that without betraying yourself?"

"I don't know, but I must—"

"Not panic."

nered as he pleased and still persuade Galen to do as he wished.

In all other matters, Galen was clear thinking, but he seemed too eager to make sure nothing bad happened to his brother. Mr. Townsend used that to his advantage in every way he could. She had had to bite her tongue more times than she wished during the uncomfortable meal. She had risen from the table as quickly as she could and come out to the garden to work. She longed to believe she was overreacting. After all, Mr. Townsend had taken that rough journey to assure himself Galen was fine. But now that he was here, Mr. Townsend acted as petulant as a child.

The clock on the mantel in the outer chamber of the bedroom chimed the hour. It was six, and her guests would be here within an hour, for the gathering was starting earlier than the functions she had hostessed in London. Skirting a low table that was edged with a trio of chairs upholstered in green, she entered the private bedchamber at an unseemly pace.

"Good evening, my lady," said Mrs. Boyd. She had arrived from Townsend Hall with Tate but had remained at Thistlewood Cottage to oversee it on behalf of Lord Townsend. If any of the servants here had been distressed by Mrs. Boyd's arrival and her assumption that they would answer to her, Phoebe had seen no sign of it.

She gave Mrs. Boyd a smile as she paused by the large oak bed. The room had plenty of room for an armoire set between the pair of windows flanked with scarlet velvet. The gray-haired housekeeper in her gown of the same drab shade was overseeing the three maids who were filling a bath set to one side on the flowered rug. Mrs. Boyd must have been spying on Phoebe in the garden in order to have everything ready.

"You are most efficient, Mrs. Boyd," she said, drawing off her borrowed work gloves and putting them on a table.

"I believe it is more that I am pleased to be of service. Lord Townsend has not been at Townsend Hall for more than a year, which is why both Tate and I took advantage of the chance to come here."

Phoebe's eyes grew wide. She had not given thought to how a household staff filled their hours when the owners were absent. Regret sifted through her. The staff at Brackenton Park had not seen her in months.

"Both Lord Townsend and I appreciate your service," she replied.

"Thank you, my lady." She chuckled, then waited until the maids had left the room. "If I may say so, I believe you made a wise decision when you offered Lord Townsend a ride in your carriage."

"Excuse me?"

She laughed again. "My lady, I know it is not my place to say anything, but Lord Townsend will tell you that I have been at Townsend Hall since he was a young pup. In that time, I have learned much about him and what he is like. You should open your eyes and see that Lord Townsend clearly adores you."

Phoebe stared at the housekeeper in amazement. Mrs. Boyd spoke as if she were Galen's mother rather than his housekeeper.

"He is a good man," Mrs. Boyd continued, "so you must be careful with his heart. I doubt if he has given it to anyone, for he thinks only of keeping his brother out of another jumble. Strong men are the most easily shattered."

Mrs. Boyd hurried out of the room before Phoebe could speak past her shock. What had persuaded the housekeeper to be so candid with her?

Going to where a pink gown decorated with gold

lace was waiting on the bed, she picked it up to discover it was one of her own from London. One of her favorite gowns, in fact. She could imagine Johnson's astonishment at a request to have her clothes taken to Sir Ledwin's, but her butler would have made certain that the unexplained order was followed exactly as she had requested.

She stared out the window that gave her a view of the rolling hills vanishing into the east. Johnson was a great ally in her work, devising tales of how she had retired early or was not receiving any callers that day. He had found ways to hide those who had escaped when the wagons they had expected were delayed. Like her butler, Galen's housekeeper was determined to do all she could to ease any stress in the lives of those she served.

And play matchmaker.

Phoebe dropped the gown back on the bed and went to the tub. A matchmaker was the last thing she needed now. Her heart was leading her into Galen's arms, when her head should be considering how she could go to London and resume her work.

She undressed and sank into the bath, sighing with pleasure. Sponging off at a bowl in a wayside inn was not the same as a real bath. She washed her hair and used the extra water to rinse it.

Regretfully, when the water grew chill, she dressed quickly in fresh smallclothes. She sat on a tufted chair and combed her hair until it hung in drying waves along her shoulders. She drew on her gown and smoothed it down her. As she began to hook it up, she realized she could not reach all the tiny hooks. The last time she had worn this, her abigail, Marie, had been there to assist. She would ring for assistance after she did her hair.

Coming to her feet, she tried to check her appearance. The glass was not at a convenient height, but, if she stood on tiptoe, she could see her reflection. Sweeping her curls up around the crown of her head, she pinned them in place with silken flowers that she took from a vase by the window. A few wisps framed her face. She adjusted the curved neckline, which dipped to offer a hint of her shoulders. Its bodice clung close before falling from the high waistline to brush her gold velvet slippers.

At a soft knock, she called, "Come in, Mrs. Boyd. Could you help me finish hooking up my gown?"

"I would be delighted," came an answer followed a masculine chuckle.

"Galen! What are you doing here?" she gasped, as she saw his smile in the glass. He was dressed in prime twig as he had been in London. His navy coat was worn over sedate gray breeches. The stripes on his waistcoat matched the lace on her gown, and his cravat was the same pristine white as his shirt.

"This is my friend's house, and he invited me to run tame through it," he said with a broadening smile.

"But this is my room, and I did not invite you to run tame through *it!*"

"I understand that, Phoebe. Let me hook you." Galen quickly closed the few Phoebe could not reach. He kept his groan silent as he pulled his fingers back before they could linger above the low neckline that revealed enough of her soft skin to urge him to undo all the hooks and toss all thoughts of caution aside.

"Thank you," she murmured.

"I am glad to help. It went much faster than the last time I hooked you up."

When she stepped away and trembled, he cursed his thoughtlessness. Even the most obtuse chucklehead would have known better than to remind her of what she had suffered when his efforts to protect her by giving her a false name had resulted in her abduction. He stroked her bare shoulders and bent forward to whisper in her ear, "Forgive me, Phoebe. I will never mention that again."

"You need not abstain from speaking of it because you think you are reminding me of it." She shuddered again. " 'Tis something I cannot forget."

"Think of something else."

"I try, but those memories refuse to be shunted aside. I see that man's horrible leer or hear the disgusting sound of his laugh, and it is as if I am there again."

He turned her to face him. Slipping his arms around her, he rested her cheek against his chest, taking care not to disturb the flowers in her hair. He stroked her back in silent solace, wishing he could find a way to turn back time to the moment when he had given her the name that had nearly caused her death.

She raised her head to look at him, and her eyes brightened with pleasure. His heart seemed to halt in midbeat as he admired her loveliness. Her chin might be tilted a bit too assertively for the preference of most men he knew, who preferred the women in their lives to be docile. Not him. He appreciated her spirit as much as her beauty. She fought to control many strong emotions, and he could not keep from savoring the fantasy of being the man to unleash them. In addition, her beauty possessed an intriguing radiance. As if his dreams had awakened to stand before him.

Stepping back a half step, Galen withdrew a long box from beneath his coat. Holding out the box that was covered with gold brocade, he said, "Take it."

"What is it?"

"You will not know until you open it, will you?"

Her nose wrinkled, and he smiled. Teasing her was delightful. He had not realized, until she climbed into his carriage and into his life, that he had become so focused on trying to oversee his brother's pursuit of entertainment that he had forgotten to think of his.

"Open it," he urged, impatiently, as she stroked the brocade.

Phoebe continued to stare at the glorious material. It reminded her of drapes in the solarium at Bracken-ton Park. She was unsure if they still hung in the sunny windows, or if the housekeeper had sold them to help pay the staff while Phoebe used her inheritance to continue her work.

"Are you going to stare at it all evening?" Galen asked.

She smiled at his impatience. That he was able to smile back without wincing pleased her more than she could have expressed. He had not complained, but she knew from talking to Roland, his valet, that the injuries Galen had endured were even more painful than he had let her know.

She raised the cover of the box. "Oh, my!" She touched the bed of emerald velvet as she stared at a spectacular gold-filigree necklace set with rubies. A pair of matching eardrops were set to one side. She traced the complicated pattern with a fingertip before looking back at him. "These are lovely."

"They will look truly lovely when you are wearing them," he said, smiling even more broadly.

"Me wearing these?"

"I thought you would fancy wearing them."

"Yes, but—"

"I surmise your household did not send any jewelry in the box that was delivered by messenger this afternoon."

"No."

"Because they worried about its safety or because you have laid it all on a shelf?"

She smiled sadly. "The cost of my attempt to save these foolhardy wretches is high, and pawnbrokers are accustomed to keeping secrets for those in the Polite World."

"Being Lady Midnight is draining you in every way."

She put her fingers to his lips. "Take care what you say, Galen."

"Take care what you do, my dear." He kissed her fingers. "A man can be tempted only so far."

"Then you should not have come to my private rooms." Her smile became more genuine.

"But how can I learn my capacity for temptation if I do not?"

Phoebe laughed. "You have a gift for nothing-sayings. No wonder, every lass in London nearly swooned when Lord Townsend spoke to her."

"Egad, I hope you are exaggerating." He lifted the necklace off the velvet. "For now, I would like to see how these look with your pretty gown."

"You are being too kind."

"Nonsense. I did not send Tate to Townsend Hall last night to retrieve these for *me* to wear. You are not the only one who considered that it would be all for the good to pretend that we had not rushed here from Town."

Stepping behind her, Galen slipped the chain around her neck and secured the latch. The gold was cool against her skin, but his fingers stroking her nape were enticingly warm. Too enticingly warm, she realized when she went to the glass and clasped the earrings on her ears. She touched the twisting of gold and gems, and tears bubbled into her eyes.

"Why are you so sad, my dear, when you look so lovely?" Galen asked.

"My father bought a necklace much like this for

my mother soon after they were married. The stones in it were emeralds."

"And it is gone?"

She nodded. "It was one of the first pieces I sold."

Galen stared at her, his mouth working. His fist struck the back of a chair. When she gasped, amazed at his reaction, he said, "Forgive me, Phoebe. I guess I am furious with myself for failing to see how much you have sacrificed."

"This jewelry is lovely, and I would rather think of what is than what was. Thank you for letting me wear these pieces. I promise I shall be very careful with them tonight." She chuckled. "And you need not worry about me taking them to a pawnbroker."

"Do whatever you wish with them." He smiled as he slipped an arm around her waist. He tapped an eardrop, then traced the angle of her cheek. "They are not a loan, Phoebe. They are a gift."

She shook her head and stepped away to escape from the magic of his touch. "I could not accept such a gift." She reached to undo the necklace.

"You must, Phoebe." He caught her hands and drew them down as he gave her a wicked grin. "I shall not do you the favor of allowing you to return them unless you are willing to do me the very special favor of my choice."

She arched a brow. "Isn't it supposed to be the other way around? If I accept, I compromise myself?"

"It would please me for you to have them. Please wear them."

She searched his face. He meant this. "Why?"

"You were not distressed when your bracelet was left behind at the inn. I could think of only two reasons. One was that you had so many baubles losing one did not matter. As that did not seem likely, I guessed the other reason must be the truth. Your jewels are paste."

"This kindness is beyond anything I expected, Galen. I have created chaos in your life, and you have never complained."

"I do believe I have complained."

"Yes, once or twice."

"Just once or twice?"

She laughed. "Once or twice a day."

"That is more accurate. Just as it is accurate that these jewels needed you to bring them back to life."

He tipped her chin up, steering her mouth to his. She combed her fingers up through his hair. Why was she resisting? She wanted his kisses and tantalizing caresses.

Before his lips could touch hers, a knock came at the outer door, and footsteps crossed the antechamber.

"Is there anything you need, Lady Phoebe? Would you—?" Mrs. Boyd froze in midstep. Her eyes narrowed and her voice became as severe as if she were disciplining a child. "My lord, what are you doing here?"

Galen bowed toward his housekeeper. "Do not shoot daggers at me, Mrs. Boyd. I assure you that I have not seduced Phoebe and certainly would not do so without her permission, which you need to have no concern about her giving."

"Galen, please!" Phoebe gasped.

Mrs. Boyd crossed her arms over her full bosom. Her mouth was straight, but her eyes twinkled as Galen's did. "My lord, Lady Phoebe will think you were raised with no manners whatsoever."

Phoebe laughed. "I would never blame anyone but Galen for his behavior, Mrs. Boyd."

"You are a wise woman." Her smile broadened. "May I say, Lady Phoebe, that you look lovely?"

"After I have the chance to say that," Galen replied before she could. "You do look lovely, Phoebe."

"Thank you." Phoebe knew she should be furious at him for acting so out of hand by coming to her room, but she could not be. His kindness warmed her heart, which she had kept so hidden from the pain of knowing she could not help all who deserved it that she had not trusted anyone with it. Now . . . She hesitated, for Galen had been right when he told her that she knew so little about him.

Mrs. Boyd stepped closer, and Phoebe thought the housekeeper was determined to keep her and Galen separated. Instead Mrs. Boyd peered at the necklace she was wearing.

"Mrs. Boyd," Galen said quietly, "you are unsettling Phoebe."

"She is wearing—"

"My gift to her."

"A gift?" Bafflement lined Mrs. Boyd's face.

"Do you think I would ask for them to be returned?" Galen laughed, but Phoebe heard an edge in his voice.

Mrs. Boyd cleared her throat, then said, "But, my lord, those are—"

"I know very well what those are, Mrs. Boyd. Please find Carr and inform him that we are on our way down to join him in greeting our guests."

"Yes, my lord." She went out, leaving the door open behind her.

Phoebe faced him. "How could you dress her down like that? She said nothing wrong."

"You are right."

"I am?" she asked, then smiled. "I did not expect you to agree so readily."

Galen took her hand and raised to his lips. "You are the pattern-card of propriety, Phoebe. No one would guess what sport you indulge in when the rest of the *ton* is involved in its flirtations."

"Galen! Please watch what you say."

"I will among our guests." He laughed. "I will apologize to Mrs. Boyd when we go downstairs. Now, I offer my apologies to you for my crude behavior."

"I would be an ungrateful wretch if I remained angry after you have been so kind."

"Kind is not what I wish to be."

"No?" She knew she was courting danger as she reached up and pushed a recalcitrant lock of hair back from his eyes.

"No." His finger glided along the chain of the necklace.

She did not dare to breathe, and she feared her heart would stop beating as his fingertip halted directly over the pendant that rested between her breasts. When his gaze held hers, she longed to give him the answer to the question she saw in his eyes.

She could not. Her life was not her own.

Something must have told him what she was thinking because he held out his arm to her. When she was about to put her hand on it, he took her fingers and drew her around to his other side.

"I will need you to help me guard my wounds from those who might be curious about how I could have done myself such injury by simply falling off my horse," he said as he settled her fingers on his arm.

"I could do no less after you played my courageous champion." This jesting was not easy when she wanted to speak of other things . . . when she wanted to speak of nothing at all as his lips stroked hers.

"Lady fair, your eager guests will soon await you." He started to bow, then winced.

"You must take care."

"As you must. I know how important this evening is to turn any suspicion away from you."

"If we make a mistake . . ." She closed her eyes and sighed.

He tipped her chin toward him. Opening her eyes, she looked up into his. "We shall not make a mistake, my dear, other than the ones we have already made."

As Phoebe went with him out into the corridor and down the steps toward the large room where they would welcome their guests, she knew she should give voice to the question taunting her. She could not. She did not want to know if he meant nothing more than the mistake he had made of giving her the wrong alias or the greater one she was making of falling in love with him.

Ten

"You look worried," Galen said as he came down to where Phoebe had been welcoming their guests to the brightly lit parlor. "You need have no fears. With Mrs. Boyd and Vogel vying to make everything perfect, you can rest assured that the staff will be beyond reproach."

Phoebe smiled. "I hope you are right."

"I almost always am." He offered his arm as he led her across the room.

Walking around one of the score of chairs and settees scattered throughout the large chamber, she chuckled. "Now *that* sounds like the Lord Townsend of rumor." She sat on a dark green settee and glanced around the room where their guests were speaking as if they had not seen each other in weeks.

All the brasses, from the window latches to the andirons, glistened from a recent polish. No dust ruined the patterns on the rugs on the stone floor. Lamps hung from the high rafters and reflected off the diamond-shaped mullions in the large windows.

Sitting beside her, Galen smiled. " 'The Lord Townsend of rumor'? That sounds most disagreeable."

"Unquestionably most disagreeable."

"Yet, here you are with that most disagreeable of men."

"So you are saying the rumors are, in fact, the truth?"

He laughed. "I doubt there has never been a rumor that did not have some hint of truth in it . . . somewhere and no matter how twisted by repetition." His fingers slipped along her cheek. "If rumor spoke of how much I wished to meet a lady who matches wits with me and delights me with her pretty lips, then that rumor has more than a hint of truth in it."

"You are trying to charm me."

"And not succeeding if you can see through my ploy."

Regret pinched Phoebe. "A ploy? Is that all this means to you?"

Galen cursed under his breath as Vogel, whose face suggested he never smiled, announced another guest. By Jove! How had his compliment, his most sincere compliment, to Phoebe been turned about to be thrown into his face?

Setting himself on his feet to follow her to where she was greeting Lord Windham and his pretty brunette wife, Nerissa, Galen winced. Blast this stupid wound! He had known that the price of playing the hero could be high, but it was now simply bothersome.

"Windham," he said with all the gusto he could bring forth, "I thought you were coming to Town for this Season."

The viscount glanced at his wife and smiled. "We decided it would be more prudent to remain close to home for the next few months."

Galen offered his congratulations on his wife's quickening to Windham, but hoped the conversation did not turn to heirs and the other obligations of a peer. His brother had harangued him about that today, asking Galen why he was wasting time with Lady Phoebe Brackenton. In Carr's opinion, she was a hopeless puritan who was more interested in her quiet evenings at home than in finding a husband.

He hoped his smile would not waver. Carr had been exasperating all day, which showed that Phoebe had the good sense to occupy herself elsewhere. Instead of staying to join the gathering tonight, Carr had wanted to go to a house not far from the Pump Room.

Galen had fought not to lose his temper as he said, "Carr, you can delay your call on Sandra for another night."

"I miss that fine woman when I am in Town."

"Do you?"

"I have sought her match through every corner of London, but I fear I have failed to meet another like her."

Tossing back his wine, Galen had set himself on his feet. "I do believe you have sought in every corner of London."

"Do not be such a prude, Galen. A man's time of freedom is short, so he would be a widgeon not to take advantage of all that is there for him to take advantage of." Carr leaned back in the chair and folded his hands under his head. "And Sandra is one of the things I do enjoy taking advantage of most." Sitting straighter, he laughed. "Join me, Galen. She would have a lass who would appeal to your taste."

"No doubt."

"Then bring along a gold coin or two and let's have an adventure that will bring you far more pleasure than this dreary assembly Lady Phoebe has devised for tonight."

"No thank you."

Carr's eyes had narrowed as he spat an oath. "She has offered you a ride to Bath, brother. Nothing more.

You need not think you owe her a duty when you have repaid her tenfold by welcoming her to stay here in Woods's house."

Galen did not recall what he replied, but it had sent his brother up to the boughs. His hope that Carr would set aside his disappointment and be waiting here when their guests arrived had been for naught.

When Phoebe spoke his name in a tone that suggested she had taken note of how his thoughts had wandered, Galen paid attention to what Windham and his wife were saying.

"Galen," Phoebe said, turning to a short man whose wife was nearly a hand's breadth taller, "this is Barry Lyttle and his wife, Matilda. Mr. and Mrs. Lyttle, our host, Lord Townsend."

It took every iota of the manners drilled into him for Galen to keep his smile a polite one as he greeted Mr. and Mrs. Lyttle. He doubted if any name had been more appropriate, for even though Mrs. Lyttle was taller than her husband, she was still the shortest woman in the room.

His urge to smile vanished when he found himself in a challenging discussion of the latest decisions to come out of Whitehall. Mr. Lyttle might be diminutive, but his brain obviously outdistanced his stature.

Phoebe watched Galen's eyes widen in amazement when Mr. Lyttle outlined his opinion on the shipping regulations that were under discussion in the Commons. Galen would quickly discover that Mr. Lyttle read every word in the newspapers he had delivered from every major city in England.

When Mrs. Lyttle tugged on Phoebe's arm, Phoebe went to stand with her by the double doors. Mrs. Lyttle opened her fan and laughed. "You should have given Lord Townsend fair warning of Mr. Lyttle's delight in having a new set of ears to air his vocabulary to."

"Now, Mrs. Lyttle," Phoebe replied, glad to be sharing an old joke when nothing else in her life remained the same as it had been when she had first met the Lyttles seven years ago. "You know Mr. Lyttle is not just talking for the sake of talking."

Mrs. Lyttle laughed with an enthusiasm that was impossible to ignore. "No, he would relish getting into a deep discussion with anyone who is ready to debate with him. I suspect he has found a mind as honed as his in Lord Townsend. Or it may be that Lord Townsend is too polite to tell Mr. Lyttle that he has no interest in the subjects that intrigue my husband."

"I collect it is the former."

She was not sure if Mrs. Lyttle heard her because Mrs. Lyttle added, "I was so pleased to hear you had decided to pay Bath a visit." Her bright blue eyes crinkled with her smile. "You should have let us know before this that you were here."

Phoebe laughed lightly. "I fear that I needed some time to recuperate from the journey down from London."

"It is a long trip." Mrs. Lyttle waved her fan and laughed. "Mr. Lyttle tries often to persuade me to go to Town, because he would like to be closer to Parliament. He would like to express his opinions in the ears of any minister who could not elude him quickly enough. I fear I would miss the camaraderie of our small group of friends here in Bath. The excitement of the Season is not enough to convince me to leave Bath." She put her hand on Phoebe's arm. "But I thought you would allow Mr. Lyttle and me to be your hosts when you visited here."

"Galen believed he owed me a duty for offering him a way to continue his trip when his carriage was damaged." Phoebe loathed the bitter taste of the lies. Somehow, before all of this erupted into such a bumble-bath, she had managed to live her dual lives without speaking too many lies. Now, every phrase she spoke seemed to be laced with falsehoods.

Phoebe pushed aside her uneasy thoughts as Galen introduced her to more of his friends who were in attendance. As the guests took their chairs to begin playing whist before dinner was served, she noticed how he glanced again and again at the doors to the terrace and the corridor. She said nothing, for she knew he was looking for his brother. Speaking of Mr. Townsend's absence now might cause Galen embarrassment.

She realized she was pacing about the room like a caged animal, but she could not sit and play cards. She tried to sit once or twice. It was impossible, and she was grateful when Lord Windham and his wife coming in from the terrace gave her the excuse to rise and go to them. She had not noticed them leaving. How rusty her skills as a hostess had become since she had begun her quest to save the almost innocent!

"I am fine," Lady Windham said, although her voice was faint and her cheeks an unhealthy shade of gray. "The room seemed a bit close, so I thought I would be wise to get some fresh air."

"If you would like, I—"

"You need do nothing." Lady Windham's smile returned. "These odd sensations pass as quickly as they come. I am fine, and I am looking forward to playing cards. Do not worry on my behalf. Hamilton is doing that enough for all of us."

Lord Windham chuckled. "Have pity on the poor father-to-be who has nothing to do but worry."

Phoebe gestured toward a settee. "There is a place if you feel lightheaded and have the need to sit."

"I think I shall be fine," he replied.

"I didn't mean . . . that is . . ."

Lady Windham slapped her husband on the arm, her color becoming more normal as she laughed. "Stop hoaxing her, Hamilton."

"Any friend of Sir Ledwin Woods must appreciate a good jest," Lord Windham said as he took a glass of wine from the nearby table. "He is known for his excellent sense of humor. She must be well accustomed to it."

Phoebe tried not to stiffen. She did not want to own that she had never met the man who owned this house. Then she realized she could be honest. "To own the truth, my lord, I have never had the privilege of meeting Sir Ledwin. He is Galen's friend."

"I understand that you are quite the heroine, my lady." Lord Windham lifted his glass in her direction. "You saved Townsend from his own folly in driving his carriage at a dangerous speed along those rough roads."

She flushed, not wanting to be false with the kindly viscount. "I did only what anyone else would have done."

"You are being too generous in your estimation of many of the people I have met."

"You are cynical, my lord."

His wife slipped her arm through his and laughed. "Do not let Hamilton's skepticism disturb you."

"Skepticism?" Lord Windham asked with a laugh of his own. "I only wish more people would be like this kindhearted lady. She stopped to help someone in need."

"As you would have," Phoebe said.

"Yes, he would have." Lady Windham smiled. "After all, that is how we met. He paused to help me when I was nearly ridden down."

"How horrible!"

Looking up at her husband with a soft smile, Lady

Windham replied, "It all worked out for the very best. Wouldn't you agree, Hamilton?"

"Yes, for the very best. If—"

"Pardon me," said a voice accompanied by an elbow that drove Phoebe back a half step.

She jumped forward so Mr. Townsend did not reel into Lady Windham and hurt her unborn child. When the odor of brandy flowed from him toward her, she scowled. He was foxed!

"Yes, do excuse him, my lord, my lady," she said as the viscount scowled at Galen's foolish brother.

Lord Windham took his wife's arm again and steered her away from Mr. Townsend who was weaving on his feet. Phoebe wanted to run after them, not only to apologize, but to prevent Mr. Townsend from engaging her in conversation when he reeked with brandy.

Mr. Townsend must not have been as drunk as she had guessed because his voice was not slurred when he said, "That was rude of them. Windham has always thought himself the better of the rest of us."

Galen crossed the room, his smile becoming a frown. He must have heard his brother's words, because Mr. Townsend took no care to lower his voice. "Carr, I am glad you have decided to join us."

"Join you?" He sniffed. "I thought I had no choice. You were quite clear in your orders."

Phoebe began, "Mr. Townsend—"

Putting his hand on her arm, Galen said, "You might be more comfortable addressing him by his given name."

She nodded, even though she would have preferred to keep as much distance as possible between her and Carr Townsend. Quietly, she said, "It would be more courteous to our guests to take this conversation elsewhere."

"Why?" Carr retorted. "Are you ashamed of any-thing you or Galen might own to in your guests' hear-ing?"

"That is enough," Galen said, his tone becoming stern. "Recall your manners, Carr."

"I shall when . . . What are you wearing?" Carr bent toward Phoebe and exclaimed, "You are wearing Grandmother's rubies!"

"Grandmother?" Phoebe gasped and looked at Galen who was frowning at his brother. He had not told her this necklace was a family heirloom. No won-der he had cut Mrs. Boyd off in the midst of her ques-tion. He must have suspected—quite rightly—that if Phoebe had known the truth, she would not have ac-cepted such a gift. Her fingers went to her throat.

Galen halted her from taking off the necklace as he had in her private chamber. Color scorched her cheeks when she remembered that. Had she lost every bit of good sense she had ever had? "Phoebe, they are mine to do with as I please." He drew her fingers away from the necklace. "And it pleases me for you to wear them."

"But, Galen . . ."

A throat was cleared.

Looking over her shoulder, Phoebe tried to ignore how every eye on the room was focused on them. Instead she turned to Vogel who said with quiet dig-nity, "My lord, you asked me to speak to you about this evening's wine."

"Thank you, Vogel." Galen took a step, then glanced at his brother. "Carr, would you check the wine with Vogel?"

"So you may put an end to this conversation?"

"So we may tend to the needs of our guests." Phoebe wanted to bite back the words as soon as they were uttered, because Carr aimed his furious gaze back at her.

Carr smiled coolly. "I would have thought, Galen, that you might have asked *me* before allowing Lady Phoebe to wear grandmother's rubies."

"Did you wish to wear them this evening?" Galen asked, his voice as chill.

Phoebe looked from one brother to the other in disbelief. She had heard Galen speak so often about how he fretted about his brother's safety. Now, when they stood face-to-face, they spoke like enemies.

Carr muttered something and stormed out of the room.

"Don't say anything, Phoebe," Galen said. Raising his voice, he called, "Dinner will be ready soon. If you will excuse us . . ." He offered Phoebe his arm and swept her out of the room before she or anyone else could speak.

The dining room was deserted. It was a lovely room. Everything shone with tender care. A chandelier was gleaming with brass and glass prisms. The candles burned brilliantly in their silver candelabra, and the china and crystal on the long mahogany table seemed to be dancing with the flames.

Galen did not give her a chance to admire it as he led her to the far side of the room and a sideboard beneath a stained-glass window. Picking up a bottle of brandy, he poured a serving into one of the waiting glasses. He downed it in one gulp.

"Say what you wish now," he said.

"It is not my place to say anything."

"Nor do you need to speak what you are so obviously thinking. Let me tell you what I am thinking. Carr is my brother. I want to keep him alive and hope that he will assume the life of a gentleman rather than a blackguard."

"You do your duty as his older brother."

"Yes."

"But nothing more?"

Galen started to answer, then poured more brandy into his glass. "Phoebe, you have your reasons for making a mess of your life. Allow me the liberty to do the same with mine."

"But I have a good reason for doing what I do!"

"Ridding yourself of guilt? It has served Carr well."

She turned to look at the doorway. "Guilt? He does not act the least bit guilty."

"I said guilt served him well. I did not say it was his guilt."

"Yours? But, Galen, you watch over him so closely. It is clear that you wish nothing to happen to him."

"Again."

"Again?"

Phoebe listened as Galen spoke of how his brother had almost died. Although she wanted to tell him that she could not see where his fault was in expecting his brother to behave with some sense of responsibility, she bit back her words. She could not fault him for his decision to help his brother. She was risking her life and her family's reputation by doing the same for strangers.

"You should take care," she said, knowing that was advice she should heed as well.

"In what way?"

"Carr is . . . He is coming to depend on you." That was the nicest way she could say what was careening through her head. "Maybe you should—"

Galen pulled her to him and gave her a tender kiss. It had not taken him long to learn this was the best and sometimes only way to silence her, she realized, but she could not push him away when she wanted him near.

He raised his mouth from hers. "Why are you prattling on about my brother? I would rather think of you."

"Of just me?"

"Of you and me."

She caressed his cheek, and his hands at her waist tightened. Hesitating, she sought words to tell him that he did not need to give her priceless gifts to make her happy. The demanding pressure of his mouth against hers was heavenly.

Carr's uneven footfalls warned Phoebe who was entering the dining room. She stepped back and out of Galen's arms, although she wanted to linger there all evening . . . and longer.

"The wine for dinner is ready," Carr announced, holding up a nearly empty glass. Sarcasm added a further chill to his voice as he added, "I appreciate your trusting me with such an important task as it appears that you do not trust me to do anything else."

Galen regarded his brother steadily. "I see you have not given up your habit of eavesdropping on otherwise private conversations."

"Eavesdropping?" He twirled the glass and smiled. "No, I was not listening to your court-promises to Lady Phoebe. I saw you sampling some of the brandy, and I thought I might as well."

"Serve yourself." Galen put his hand on Phoebe's arm and turned her toward the table. "Phoebe and I—"

"Phoebe and *you?* Is there something you were remiss in not telling me?"

With a growl of a curse he would not have wanted Phoebe to hear, he grasped his brother's arm. He was surprised when Carr did not protest. Then he realized that his brother wanted to speak to him, that everything Carr had done since coming into the parlor had been aimed at provoking Galen so they could speak alone.

He looked back at Phoebe. Her smile was brittle, and her eyes snapped with fury before she went to the doorway as the Lyttles appeared in it. Was she furious at him? He was trying to protect her from Carr's untoward behavior. Blast his brother! And blast Phoebe for not understanding.

"What is so important?" he asked.

Carr's eyes widened, then his mouth straightened. "You allowing that woman to act as if she is your beloved when you could not have known her a fortnight ago."

"You don't believe in love at first sight?"

"No, and neither do you. Lust? Mayhap. Love? No. By King Harry, Galen, you cannot disregard what you must have heard in Town about her."

"What I have heard is that she is kindhearted and pretty mannered."

"She is blasted old," Carr grumbled. "She must be a half dozen years past twenty. You should consider that young miss I introduced you to at Almack's. Now, *she* would make you a worthy wife."

"I am not presently looking for a wife."

"Does she realize that?"

"Yes."

Carr's lips curled into a superior smile, the one that Galen had always despised, for he knew his brother was about to jump to the wrong conclusion. Carr proved him right by saying, "Now I understand why you have no interest in coming with me to pay a call on Sandy and her girls. You have a marquess's daughter to warm your bed."

"You insult Lady Phoebe."

"What are you going to do? Call me out for grass before breakfast?"

"Don't be ridiculous."

"I am not the ridiculous one. I am not the one who has her wearing our grandmother's rubies like a placard announcing her place in this house."

Galen clasped his hands behind his back before he could reach out and shake some sense into his brother's brandy-drenched brain. "Did you ever give credence to the idea that her own jewelry was stolen on our way here?"

"So you lent her Grandmother's rubies?"

"No, I gave them to her."

Carr sputtered with fury. "How could you do something so want-witted?"

Galen's answer was forestalled when Phoebe said with a lightness he doubted any of their guests would guess was forced, "You two gentlemen should realize that some of the other gentlemen would appreciate a chance to share your brandy and your conversation."

"I leave you to your *lady*," Carr said with a sneer. "I can see you are so fascinated with her fascinating arts that you were too busy to send a carriage for me to the Little Lost Lamb a few nights ago."

Phoebe flinched. Not at the insults Carr spoke, but how easily he might reveal that all she and Galen had said tonight was based on lies.

When Galen slipped her arm through his and went to the table where their guests were listening agog, she knew her face was the same deep red as the rubies. Somehow, she was not sure how, she restarted the conversation. The guests soon were busy discussing every topic that appealed to them, but she was aware of their glances at her and Galen and his disagreeable brother who sat across the table from her. Carr ignored her, and, for that, she was grateful.

The evening came to a close shortly after midnight. When the last guest took his leave, Galen's shoulders sagged with the fatigue he had hidden throughout the gathering. His smile faded, and the lines of pain returned to his face.

"Sit," Phoebe said as she steered him toward a chair in the parlor.

A maid appeared with a tray and a single glass. Thanking her, Phoebe took it and held it out to Galen.

"Hot milk?" he asked with a chuckle.

"To help you sleep."

"I believe you are conspiring with Mrs. Boyd, Phoebe."

She sat on a stool by his chair. "I believe she worries that you are going to overdo and injure yourself more." Smiling, she said, "Drink your hot milk."

With a grimace, he took a sip. "What is that I taste?"

"Cinnamon and sugar. It makes the hot milk easier to swallow."

Taking her hand, he smiled. "You will spoil me."

"As you spoil your brother?"

He set the glass on a nearby table and came to his feet. "I should have guessed you had an ulterior reason for hovering over me. You barely know my brother." He laughed humorlessly. "By Jove, to own the truth, you barely know *me*. I do not need to endure a lecture from you."

"So you would rather let your brother lambaste you with his selfish demands?" Slowly she stood. "I know it is not my place to speak so."

"It is not."

"You have come to my rescue more than once."

"So now you intend to rescue me from my own brother?" He reached for the glass, then grimaced and set it back on the table.

"You act as if you were his father and he the ill-behaved son."

"I am his brother, and I am responsible for him."

"Why?"

His eyes narrowed. "Why?"

"Yes, that is what I wish to know. Why do you feel responsible for him? He is a man full grown. He needs to learn to be responsible for himself."

"Like those petty criminals you free from being transported?" He strode to the door and put his hand on the knob. "You speak of me being a beef-head for watching out for my brother, yet you watch out for those who should have known better than to lift a purse or steal a hen. I have not interfered in your skimble-skamble, Phoebe. Do not interfere with my family obligations."

Reaching up, she yanked off the necklace. Its latch broke and skittered across the floor. She pressed the necklace into his hand. Walking away, she realized she still wore the earrings. She paused and undid them. She went back to where he still stood and dropped them into his hand.

"And what is this performance supposed to mean?" he asked.

She faltered when she saw how the lines of pain were deepening around his mouth. Mayhap he was speaking out of the anguish that must still be bothering him with every breath he took. Wanting to have sympathy for him, she knew she would only be hurting him more if she did.

Quietly she said, "It means tomorrow I will be looking for another place to live until I can return to London. I will not stay here and watch your brother manipulate you and speak carelessly and betray both of us."

"Carr was in his cups. He was not seeing clearly."

"But I am."

He threw the necklace and earrings onto the chair where he had been sitting. "I do not believe you."

"What?"

"I do not believe you are going to find another place to reside in Bath." He seized her shoulders. "I believe you are planning to return to London as soon as possible. You accuse my brother of foolishness and yet you will go and risk your life to save strangers."

"I did not accuse your brother of foolishness." She jerked herself out of his grasp. Again she nearly faltered, knowing that she would not have been able to free herself unless he was weakened by his wound. She lifted her chin. She could not let sympathy for him keep her from saying what she must. "Carr is very smart. He is using you to get exactly what he wants, and what he wants is to keep you from paying more attention to me than to him."

She rushed out of the room before she could say more. She tried to erase the image of Galen's stricken face from her memory. It was impossible, and she doubted if she ever could.

Eleven

Mrs. Boyd bustled about Phoebe's bedchamber, oddly silent. There was no need for conversation. Phoebe was well aware of the housekeeper's dismay at last night's brangle, but Phoebe was as reticent. To speak of what she and Galen had said would only distress Mrs. Boyd more.

"I am going out to take the air," Phoebe said when she could no longer endure Mrs. Boyd's anxious glances.

"A fine idea, my lady. A brisk walk always helps me regain my perspective." A tremulous smile tried to form on her lips.

"You are right." She had lost her perspective. She was worried too much about Galen when she should be thinking of her work in London. Without Jasper who loitered on the docks and alerted her when a ship was ready to sail for Australia, she could not know if she had missed the chance to help.

Bidding Mrs. Boyd a good day, Phoebe put on her bonnet and went to the front door. She took her parasol from a footman before stepping out into the afternoon sunshine. She looked across the river to the curving streets of Bath. The wisest course of action would be to call on the Lyttles whose house was only a few blocks from the Royal Crescent. As she crossed the Pulteney Bridge, she turned in the other direction. She did not want to call on her friends until her emotions were more firmly under control.

Walking toward the Abbey whose spires rose into the sky, Phoebe grimaced as she recalled how silly her heart had been when Galen offered her that lovely necklace to wear. She had dared to believe his heart might have been touched by her as hers had been by him. Mayhap she should not have returned the jewelry as she did. Yet, how much easier it would have been if he had given the necklace and earrings to her only as a prelude to seduction.

Mrs. Boyd had said last night that Galen adored her. That might be true, but he concerned himself first with keeping his brother out of trouble, and she should do the same, thinking solely of finding a way to continue her interrupted work.

Phoebe strolled past the Pump Room, not pausing as she wandered through the curving streets of the city. Lost in her thoughts and wishing she could stumble upon an answer to solve all these problems, she paid little attention to the shopwindows she passed.

She should return to London. Right away. Even if the rumors of Lady Midnight were sweeping through Town, she could take care that no one connected those tales with her.

She sighed. Jasper was safe at Brackenton Park, but she knew Johnson remained at Grosvenor Square and was still worried about her safety. Her butler would have sent her a message to come back to London if he believed she would be safe in Town.

The rumble of thunder intruded on Phoebe's uneasy thoughts. Her steps faltered when she discovered that she did not know where she was or how she had gotten there. The houses were no less elegant than most of the buildings in Bath, but she was not sure where she was in the city. The terraced houses edging the walk-way prevented her from seeing any landmarks.

Lightning flashed across the darkening sky, and Phoebe turned to go back the way she had come, hoping she could reach the Pump Room before the storm arrived. She could wait there during the storm. Once the rain passed, she would return to Thistlewood Cottage. Then . . .

"Oh!" she gasped when a man lurched toward her, blocking her way.

He was dressed well, but from the reek coming from him, she guessed he had been giving a bottle of blue ruin a black eye. He stank worse than Carr had last night. She hoped he was not as aggravating. She tried to walk around him. He stepped directly into her path again.

"Are you lost, darling?" His words fired a miasma of liquor-drenched breath at her.

"I can find my way. Thank you." Her fingers tightened on her parasol, but she closed it. Another clap of thunder warned that she would have been wiser to bring an umbrella. "If you will excuse me, I shall bid you a good day."

He took an uneven step toward her, and she backed away. With a drunken chuckle, he said, "There is no need to hurry away, darling. I will be certain that you are taken home after."

"After?" she asked, her eyes narrowing. "After what?"

His arm snaked around her waist. "After you give me a kiss, darling."

"I do not think so!" she retorted, irritated by his assumption that she would submit willingly. Raising her chin, she tried to hold his drunken stare. It kept sliding away, as if he could not endure for her to see how altogethery he was.

"You do not think so?" He started to release her, then his hands gripped her shoulders painfully as she heard the astounding sound of laughter from behind her.

She looked back to see two other men grinning drunkenly at her. With a smile of her own, she struck the man on the arm with her parasol. He yelped and released her. When his friends shouted, she fled as lightning flared through the afternoon sky. Pounding feet on the cobbles behind her told her that she was being chased. She must find somewhere to hide from these foxed fools. The pungent odor of the waters that came into the Pump Room grew stronger. She must be getting closer to it. Once she reached there, the members of the Polite World who were taking the waters would halt these scoundrels.

Phoebe rushed down an alley and hid in the indentation behind a chimney. Her heartbeat roared in her ears, and each breath burned in her side. When the men raced past, she slumped back against the wall behind her. She counted to twenty to give the men time to be far along the street before she emerged.

A triumphant bellow snapped her head to her left to see a man's silhouette at the end of the alley. She pushed aside laundry that would soon be drenched and jumped over children's toys. Coming to a dead end, she retraced her steps, hoping her pursuers had lost interest in following her when a storm was coming along the river. Her slippers became filthy as she rushed between the pale yellow walls, and she stopped wiping her loosened hair out of her eyes.

She stepped out of a narrow alley and onto a street. She sighed when she saw the unmistakable lines of the Bath Abbey past several rows of houses. She was

farther from Thistlewood Cottage than she had
guessed. When a lightning bolt darted between two
clouds, she cringed.

"Come in before it storms," called a soft alto voice.

Phoebe saw a woman standing in the open door of
a house to her left. "Thank you." She rushed up the
trio of steps and into an elegant foyer. It glistened with
freshly polished wood and gilt on the walls. Overhead,
the ceiling was painted with a pastoral scene. That
tranquility vanished when light flashed into the entry
followed almost immediately by thunder that shook
the house.

"Close the door, Leonard," the woman said, motioning to a footman as rain pelted the floor. The
woman's finely carved features matched the graciousness of her home. Silver in her blond hair flattered
her youthful face. Full curves were visible above the
dress which dipped unfashionably low across her
bosom. "You arrived just in time, young lady."

"I appreciate your kindness to a stranger." Phoebe
smiled.

"We are accustomed to offering a welcome to
strangers here." She laughed and glanced toward a
wide doorway opposite the stairs. A half-dozen women
were arranged in a lovely tableau on settees in the
grand room.

"I did not mean to intrude on your callers."

"These? They are not my callers. They live here."

Phoebe could not pull her gaze away from the magnificent room. The women had hair of every shade
from as dark as Galen's to sunset red. Two were quite
short, but the rest were tall. There was little resemblance between any of them, except that they had chosen gowns very similar to the one worn by the woman
here in the foyer.

Realizing the woman was watching her closely, Phoebe said, "Forgive me. I did not mean to be rude."

"Rude?"

"To be staring so."

"We are not a family, if that is what you find baffling." The woman chuckled again. "I suspect from your puzzlement that you are not looking for anything but shelter."

"Yes."

"That is what I feared."

"Feared?" She turned to the door. The men who had chased her were not visible through the frosted glass. "May I ask what else you would think I might be seeking here?"

"Work."

"Work?" Thunder shook the house again, and a horrible sense of foreboding struck Phoebe as she saw the woman's smile broaden.

"I have a full household, as you can see, but I would be willing to take on a girl as lovely as you. My patrons like freshness."

"Pardon me?" Her breath caught in her throat. This was not sanctuary. This must be a brothel. Backing toward the door, she bumped into a bushy plant in a large container. "I appreciate your kindness, but you are clearly busy, so I should take my leave."

Phoebe threw open the door. Thunder boomed, and rain scattered across the cobbled street. The footman mumbled an apology before closing the door again.

"There is no need to be so shy," the woman said, putting her hand on Phoebe's arm. "I see you are not looking for a place in my house. What a pity! With your beauty, you soon would be a favorite here."

Knowing she was blushing, Phoebe squared her shoulders. She had seen harlots on the docks in London, but she had never thought she would be speaking to a Cyprian here in Bath. If she had been able to confront the low life on the docks, she should be able to handle this situation with aplomb. Mayhap she had never learned how to address a harlot, but she would not be discourteous.

"May I ask you to call me a chair?" Phoebe kept her fingers tightly around the handle of her parasol. Mayhap then no one would take note of how they trembled.

"It will not be easy to obtain a chair until the weather clears." The woman smiled. "I am Sandra Raymond, and this is my house. What is your name?"

"Lady Phoebe Brackenton."

"*Lady?*" Her laugh filled the foyer. "You are obviously not accustomed to being in a place like this. Mayhap I should send a boy to have someone come to escort you home. That would be much quicker than trying to get one of those lazy lads to come out in the rain."

Phoebe nodded, increasingly uncomfortable. She had never guessed that anyone in a brothel would behave with such grace. However, she had to own that she had never given any consideration to what the residents of such a place would be like.

"Tell me to whom I should send the message," Miss Raymond said, her smile still warm.

Phoebe did not hesitate. If she knew Lord Windham better, she would send for him. Mr. Lyttle would come, but the gabble-grinding man might not be able to keep the story of this rescue to himself. She had no idea what street they lived on. That left only one other person. The person she had learned to count on coming to her rescue when she needed a friend who could keep a secret. She could not worry that their most recent words had been spoken in anger.

"Galen Townsend," Phoebe replied. "He is staying at—"

Miss Raymond's smile grew very wide. "I know where Lord Townsend is staying in Bath." She gave Phoebe an assessing look. "So you are the woman who has stolen Lord Townsend's heart."

"Stolen his heart?" She wanted to ask how Miss Raymond knew that. How fanciful could she be? She had not stolen Galen's heart.

"Not that I should be surprised. Trust Lord Townsend to choose the prettiest lady to come to Bath in years."

"You know Galen? I mean—" She stopped, embarrassed.

Miss Raymond reached for a bellpull. "I hope you do not feel as uneasy as you look, Lady Phoebe. I shall tell you the truth about Lord Townsend and me. Then you shall not need to fret that he has been unfaithful. I understand some women can be very jealous."

"I am not jealous of anything about Galen." She forced her fingers to loosen on the parasol so Miss Raymond would not guess how she was lying. Telling tales seemed to be getting more difficult with each one she spoke. "It is not my place to be." Sudden tears filled her eyes. After the argument with Galen, she truly had no reason to have anything to do with his private life, especially with his life in this brothel. She looked around herself and shivered even as grief pulsed through her.

"Let me lay any fears you might have to rest, my lady. Lord Townsend and I have had a long relationship, because of his brother."

"Brother?"

"Carr Townsend is a very dear friend." She laughed. "Last night, during his most recent call, he mentioned that Lord Townsend had encountered a woman who may well have done what no other had."

"Done?" Phoebe was unsettled to discover she had been the focus of gossip in this brothel.

"Surely you must know that, before now, no other woman has convinced Lord Townsend to fall in love with her." She turned to a young girl dressed in a prim dress and apron. "Lois, tell Herb to go to Lord Townsend's house." She went to a nearby table and pulled out a drawer. Writing quickly on a small slip of paper, she added, "Make sure Herb understands this message is to go directly into Lord Townsend's hand. No one else."

"Yes, Miss Raymond." The girl took it and rushed away.

"My lady," Miss Raymond continued, "Lord Townsend is certain to come as soon as he receives the message, but you must understand that I am expecting other callers."

"I can wait . . . somewhere." She glanced at the windows where rain splattered.

"Of course. I have a small room upstairs where you may stay out of sight until Lord Townsend can send a carriage for you." Miss Raymond chuckled. "To own the truth, my lady, I am pleased you have no interest in offering me competition. If my patrons were to see you here, I daresay they would be disappointed with my girls." Her nose wrinkled. "Even when you are so disheveled."

Phoebe put her hand up to her hair. It was cascading from her bonnet and down over her shoulders. Seeing her reflection in a pier glass set by the parlor door, she wanted to gasp in horror. It was a wonder that Miss Raymond had opened her door to her instead of letting her remain outside to continue her vagabond ways.

"What happened to you?" Miss Raymond's voice remained sympathetic.

"A drunken lout waylaid me. When I informed him that I did not want his kisses, he and his companions were quite rude."

Miss Raymond's expression became grim. "There are too many rakes who believe a woman walking alone must be interested in their company. You were fortunate to avoid these rogues, Lady Phoebe." Her smile returned. "If you will come with me, you can wait upstairs."

Phoebe started to follow, then faltered. She might risk her reputation by going deeper into this house. If her reputation was blemished, she could find herself unwelcome among the *ton* in London. Then it would be so difficult to create an alibi for herself so she could help the poor unfortunates who should not be banished to the far side of the world.

"My lady?" asked Miss Raymond, motioning again to the stairs.

"I shouldn't!" Realizing she sounded ungrateful when Miss Raymond wished only to help her, she added, "I believe it would be simpler for me to wait in the kitchen or some other place which is out of the way."

Again Miss Raymond's laugh billowed through the foyer. "Do not fret. No one shall learn that you took refuge here but Lord Townsend. However, if you stay here on the ground floor, I can assure you that plenty of my callers will see you."

A knock on the door seconded Miss Raymond's warning. Grasping her skirt, Phoebe rushed up the stairs in Miss Raymond's wake. She looked back, but the footman did not open the door. As she reached the shadows that were draped like fine netting through the upper hall, she heard the footman greet a man whose name she instantly recognized.

"You must forget what you might chance to overhear here," Miss Raymond murmured. "That is the first rule of this demimonde you have entered."

"I shall." Phoebe doubted if she had ever told a more blatant lie. Although she would like to put every ignoble moment out of her mind forever, she suspected she would never be able to forget any of this.

She followed Miss Raymond into a sparsely furnished room. None of the richness of downstairs was here. However, when lightning flashed, she saw the wood floors were well polished, and a single painting eased the emptiness of the walls. The room contained a chest, a single wooden chair, and a narrow bed.

Phoebe choked and turned back to the door before the thunder resounded along the street, sending rain more fiercely against the room's sole window.

Miss Raymond put a hand on her arm. "What is wrong, my lady?"

"I cannot stay *here!*" Phoebe cried.

"Do not fret," she said again. "This room is not where a patron would be entertained. One of the maids sleeps here." She swept out a hand. "I would not take you to one of my girl's rooms. Goodness, do you always blush so much?"

"Only when I am in a brothel."

Miss Raymond stared at Phoebe, then laughed again. "Now I understand why you have distressed Carr so much. He prefers his women without a hint of astuteness."

"I thought you said he was a friend of yours."

"How gracious you are, my lady, to think of my feelings. Carr Townsend accepts my intelligence with some reluctance because he knows he must to be welcomed here."

Despite the fact that Sandra Raymond could guarantee her ruin, Phoebe appreciated the kindness of this brash woman who was trying to make her comfortable in this whole absurd situation. "It seems that you have convinced him to heed good sense."

"As much as one can, I suspect." She did not pause as she added, "Why don't you rest, Lady Phoebe? When Lord Townsend arrives, I shall send him directly up to you. I will be busy with my patrons by then, so allow me to say good-bye now."

"Thank you so much." She was not certain what else she could—or should—say. No lessons in etiquette had prepared her for *this*.

"No need for gratitude, my lady. Just one thing." She paused in the doorway and said with studied nonchalance, "If you decide you do not want Lord Townsend, do send him to me. His brother's stories of him intrigue me greatly." She winked and closed the door before Phoebe could respond to such an outrageous comment.

Sitting in the chair by the window, Phoebe let a smile spread slowly across her face. Galen was sure to be shocked when he received the message to come *here* to retrieve one errant Phoebe Brackenton.

She hoped he would not ignore her call for help.

Twelve

The nearly spent candle threw distorted shadows on the walls when a gentle kiss roused Phoebe. A soft smile parted her lips as she looked up into Galen's face, which warmed her dreams each night. She brought him closer. When his arm swept beneath her, lifting her against his strong chest, she welcomed his beguiling lips. Something creaked softly as he pressed closer to her. Scintillating sparks burst from his fingers where he caressed her back.

"You came for me, Galen," she murmured as his mouth traced the pulse along her neck.

His laugh rumbled through her as the thunder had, dangerous, yet exciting. "Did you think I would be unable to resist the invitation to call on the virtuous Phoebe Brackenton at a brothel?"

"Galen!"

His smile broadened as his gaze raked her face with unfettered desire. "What? Are you telling me that you are a reluctant harlot? If you choose to meet me at Sandra Raymond's house, you are supposed to give me pleasure, not problems."

"I did not *choose* to meet you here!"

"Is that so?" He laughed and brushed her lips with a fiery kiss before sitting on the edge of the bed. Holding out his hand, he brought her up to sit beside him. "You must be the most trusting woman in England. Next time you fall asleep in an unlocked room in a brothel—"

"Miss Raymond assured me this is not a room where . . ." Hating that her face burned with embarrassment even as his smile widened, she hurried to say, "This is a maid's room."

"True, and a maid was within. You are fortunate that I was the first to try the latch. Another man might not have been put off easily from relieving you of your virginity."

"Is that so?" she mocked in a tone as sarcastic as his. "Then I am pleased, Lord Townsend, that you have been a gentleman."

"A gentleman?" With a growl, he shoved her back into the thin pillows. He silenced her astonishment as he captured her lips. When she gasped at his intensity, his tongue boldly explored each hidden delight of her mouth. An ache of longing seared through her, demanding satiation. As his tongue flicked along her cheek and sought the curves of her ear, she tightened her arms around him, swept into this tempest of passion.

"Phoebe," he murmured against her ear, "you label me a gentleman, but I consider myself want-witted."

She opened her eyes as she clasped his face between her hands. "No more than I am for being so angry at you over something so insignificant."

"I know I turn a blind eye too often when it comes to Carr's misdeeds, but I have come to believe a small amount of trouble is better for him to involve himself in rather than a large amount of trouble." He chuckled. "As you seem to find yourself in large amounts of trouble far too regularly, my dear. This is the third time I have come to your rescue."

"They say the third time is the charm."

"That is not true." His smile vanished as candid longing filled his eyes. "I have been charmed by you since the moment we first spoke."

A thrill of exquisite pleasure swept aside everything but the longing for his touch as his fingers slipped down her back. "As I have been by you."

"And I am wasting this time by being a gentleman." The twinkle in his eyes became as mischievous as any expression his brother ever wore. "Do you want a gentleman, Phoebe, or a man who will teach you to free the passions you cannot hide?"

"You always ask such difficult questions." Her words became a sigh as his mouth drifted along her neck again.

"Is this one so difficult?"

"No," she murmured, drawing his mouth back toward hers.

"I like your answer, but not here." With a sudden laugh, he released her.

In disbelief, she stared at him. When she saw his grin, she began to smile also. "What a vexing man you are!"

"So you have already said on more than one occasion." He stood and held out his hand. "I think we should continue this conversation in more genteel surroundings. Miss Raymond's lad took to heart her insistence that the message be delivered only into my hand, and he waited several hours for me to return home."

Phoebe glanced toward the window to discover that a lazy twilight was darkening the sky. Any remnants of the storm had long vanished, and she realized her nap had not been a short one. That was no surprise, for sleep had evaded her often during the past week. "I had no idea it was so late."

"Late enough for many of Miss Raymond's patrons to be downstairs." Laughing, he said, "Speaking with a few of them delayed me from getting up here as swiftly as I had wanted. Every minute I was caught up in the discussion of gossip, I feared was the very one when you would set your good sense aside and decide you had waited long enough. Then you would have come down the stairs, looking all tousled and with your reputation in tatters."

"I believe I am wiser than that."

"Except when you get an idea in your head that you need to be somewhere to help someone. Then you have the wisdom given to a goose."

She could not argue with that. "But if I cannot go down the stairs, then how will I be able to leave? If I stay here all night, I certainly will be shunned by the Polite World. If that happens, I—"

Galen started to put his finger against her lips, then decided his lips would do much better to hush her concerns. The silken warmth of her hair spiraling around him as he drew her into his arms was intoxicating. If he pressed her back against the mattress again, would she push him away or pull him closer?

With a moan, he released her. His voice was raw with the need he fought to restrain. "Let's go. If we stay here, I will have to pay Miss Raymond for the use of this room."

"Pay?" Her eyes grew wide; then she laughed. "I think you are presuming far too much, Galen Townsend."

"It is easy to presume too much when one is alone with a lovely woman in a bordello." He ran his finger along her shoulder, letting it slip beneath the rumpled silk of her sleeve. When she gasped gently, he stroked her fragrant skin. "I must own, however, that I do not need to be here to have such thoughts."

"About what happened last—"

This time, he put his finger against her lips. If he was addle-witted enough to kiss her again, he was uncertain if he could stop with only the kisses that sent an aching hunger through him that threatened to strip him of all reasonable thought. "Before we delve into matters of the past, we need to think about your future and getting you out of here." He picked up her slippers and frowned as he saw the stains on them. "Then you can answer my questions of how you came to be here and what happened to these." Kneeling, he put her slippers on her feet.

She laughed. "Can it be you wish to be my charming prince?"

"I daresay I have done all required of such a gallant wretch by rescuing you from a life as a Cyprian." He stood and tweaked her nose. "It is quite time for the princess to return to her castle, although you are a very bedraggled princess."

He brought her to her feet. He knew he should resist, but as her soft laugh washed over him, he tugged her into his arms once more. There was nothing teasing about the kiss he placed on her lips. As her hands stroked his shoulders, he sought deep in her mouth for his pleasure. Soft puffs of her breath caressed his tongue as he fought his yearning to satisfy his need for her.

Gruffly, he murmured as he released her so quickly that she was rocked back on her heels, "Let's go."

Dazed by the power his kisses had on her, Phoebe said nothing as Galen led her out of the room. Voices rose from the lower floor, and she choked back a gasp when she heard footfalls on the stairs from the foyer.

"This way," Galen whispered.

She nodded as she matched his hurried steps toward the back of the house. When she saw another, far simpler staircase, she wanted to crow with relief. Her outburst would only draw attention to them, so she bit her lip as they went down the back stairs.

A motion at the base released a soft cry that she could not hold back. Galen put his hand on her arm. When she looked up at him, he wore a taut smile. She wished she knew what it meant.

Her steps slowed as a burly man with a thatch of startlingly red hair stood and faced them. His hand settled on a bludgeon at his side. Then he lifted his hand away. "Lord Townsend, Miss Raymond said I was to let you and—I was to let you out."

"Thank you." Galen's voice was clipped.

The man unlocked the door and held it open. "Good night."

Hearing the door being locked behind them, Phoebe glanced back as they walked through the narrow garden. No garish lights from Miss Raymond's house announced its use in this elegant neighborhood. It might have been as respectable as its neighbors. She wondered if the other houses were brothels as well or if their residents even had an idea of what was transpiring in Miss Raymond's house. With the many gatherings that the *ton* reveled in, the arrivals and departures at her door might not be noticed. Or it might simply be that the neighbors ignored what was happening in their midst.

Galen's chuckle startled her.

"What is so funny?" she asked.

"I should say all of this, because I doubt if I have ever been in such a ridiculous predicament." He drew her hand within his arm. "There is some comfort in knowing that that bully-back was even more uncomfortable than I was."

"Bully-back?"

"A strong man who oversees the doors of a brothel."

He laughed. "I am surprised you have not heard the term during your excursions to the less well lit regions of London. Arlo ensures that none of Miss Raymond's patrons leave without settling their accounts with her."

"Arlo is the man by the back door?"

He nodded. "He is a well-trained minion. He did everything he could not to acknowledge you. I am sure that Miss Raymond told him that he should not recall anything about you."

Phoebe put her other hand on his arm as well. "I believe I have you to thank for that."

"Actually you have Miss Raymond to thank for that. Think of the reputation her house would get if it was learned that ladies were welcomed there. No gentleman would visit again for fear of seeing his wife at the same time he was calling on his convenient." He laughed. "She would be out of business in no time."

"You seem to know a lot about schools of Venus."

He put his hand over hers. Although she could not see his face well in the shadows, she guessed he was grinning. "To most ladies, I would give the quick response that my past is undoubtedly more sullied than yours. However, with you, it seems you have a gift for misdeeds and skirting the parameters of the Polite World that even my brother cannot claim."

She started to retort but swallowed the words when she heard the regret that came into his voice each time he spoke of Carr Townsend. She said only, "Thank you, for rescuing me."

"It seems to be becoming a habit, but I must own that I have reveled in playing the dashing hero for you this evening." He ran his finger across her lips. "The prize for my bravery was sweet, and this time I did not have to fight anyone to save you. I only had to fight myself."

She gazed up at him. "You know that you should

not be complicating your life more with my predicaments."

"I know."

"You have enough to worry about with your brother."

"I know."

"If I were discovered to be Lady Midnight, then you could be ruined with me."

"I know." He took her hands and folded them between his. "Both of us know that, but it does not change anything, does it?"

"It must change everything. I will not stop what I am doing, and I will not endanger you more."

Leading her toward the street, he said, "This is better discussed at Thistlewood Cottage." He paused before stepping into the circle of light from the streetlamp. Looking both ways, he smiled. "No one, but Tate with the carriage. Let's go before someone chances to see you."

Phoebe clenched her hand on his arm as she saw the carriage waiting beyond the light. She had to slow her feet, although she wanted to scurry to the carriage and into it and back to the familiar house on the other side of the bridge. The temptation to laugh was almost too much when she thought of how Mrs. Boyd had applauded her idea of a walk so she might sort out her priorities. Now she was more confused.

As Galen held out his hand to assist her into the carriage, she was startled when his young coachee asked, "Are you all right, Lady Phoebe?"

"Do not speak her name here," Galen hissed.

Tate's chagrin was visible even in the darkness beyond the streetlamp. "Forgive me. I did not mean to do anything to endanger the lady."

"I realize that." Galen clapped him on the shoulder. "Just take us home, Tate."

"Yes, my lord."

As she stepped into the carriage and lowered herself gratefully to the familiar seat, she said, "Tate, I am fine. Thank you for asking."

He tipped his cap to her and grinned before he swung up into the box.

When Galen sat beside her on the thick-cushioned seat, Phoebe needed no more than his finger against her cheek to persuade her to lean her head on his shoulder. She wanted to be beside him like this. Once they returned to the house, the brangle might begin anew. For now, she would delight in this stolen moment.

"Tell me," he whispered against her hair. "Tell me how you came to be at Miss Raymond's."

She did. His shoulder stiffened beneath her cheek when she spoke of trying to walk off her anger with him. It became more rigid than the walls of the carriage as she related her encounter with the rude men but relaxed again when she told him of the welcome from the storm that Miss Raymond had offered her.

"She was very kind, Galen."

"A surprise?"

"Yes, but because I know so little of the demimonde that everything and everyone within it would surprise me. Were you astonished to receive a message from her about me?"

"Astonishment?" He chuckled. "That would be a mild description of what I felt. Any message I have previously received from Miss Raymond has been about Carr."

"Yes, she mentioned they were friends."

"Friends?" He laughed again.

"Her word, not mine."

He framed her face with his wide hands. "What is it about you, Phoebe Brackenton, that makes everyone want to look after you? Could it be that your heart is so full of kindness that no one else can ignore it?"

"You are asking silly questions."

Laughing when he did, she wanted to tell him to stop talking and to kiss her again. She should be pleased that he was showing good sense, even if she was not. If things had been different, she would gladly have risked her heart in its pursuit of his. But things were not different.

"Phoebe?" he asked gently, breaking into her thoughts.

As she looked up, he tilted her mouth under his, and she wondered if he had guessed what she had yearned for or if it was simply that he wanted the same. He leaned her across him, facing him, as his fingers blazed a path of pleasure around her waist. Taking care not to touch the bandaging she could feel beneath his waistcoat, her fingers stroked the wealth of muscles on his chest before rising to his nape and the warm skin she longed to explore.

"I was wrong," he said, "to be so vexed with you last night when you offered your opinion."

"I am sorry, too. I should not have thought I had a right to speak so. Carr is *your* brother, and he is your concern."

"And you are a woman who cares too much about everyone she meets. My dear, you really have to stop trying to right all the wrongs in the world."

"What is wrong now is that we are speaking of this when I wish . . ." Her words became a soft moan when he lifted her hand and pressed his mouth to her palm. Her eyes closed so she could savor the thrill of his kiss. Even through her dress and shift, she could sense the escalating heat of his body. Her hand against his back held him near.

Still holding her hand, he tipped her chin up with

her own finger as he smiled. "We have wasted too much time." He kissed her lightly.

"Yes."

"Let me make it up to you," he continued to her growing frustration. She did not understand why he was prattling when she longed for his kisses. "May I escort you to Her Grace's soirée tomorrow evening?"

It took a pair of heartbeats before his words reached her befuddled brain. "Yes," she whispered. At the moment, there was little she would have denied him. "Anything, Galen."

"Anything?" He chuckled.

She leaned her face against his shoulder again. "Almost anything."

"Then take back the rubies, Phoebe. I had them repaired, and I would like to see you wear them tomorrow night." From a pocket in the door, he withdrew the brocade case and placed it in her hands.

"Carr will not like this."

"They do not belong to Carr. They belong to me." His hand curved along her shoulder. "I had thought they would belong to you, but you do not seem to want them."

"Such a gift is too overmastering. It creates a debt that is not comfortable between us."

As the carriage crossed the bridge, he said, "I do not want a debt—or anything else—between us."

"Galen!"

He laughed. "I do like that feigned shock in your voice."

" 'Tis not feigned."

He kissed her deeply, then whispered, "You may try to hoax yourself, Phoebe, but you cannot hoax me. Not when I taste the longing on your lips."

"But that does not change what I must do."

"Ah, there is that ladyish tone again, giving me a

most polite dressing-down." He leaned her face back against his chest. "I understand your anxiety now, which is why I am not *giving* them to you. I want you to wear them tomorrow night. Wear them for me."

She looked from the box to his eyes, which were dark, glistening pools in the light from a lamp they were passing. "Thank you. I will wear them."

"No, do not thank me. Those gems were dead until you gave them life. It is as if they have been waiting for you. Do not deny them or me your beauty."

"You need not ply me with compliments when I said I would do as you want."

His laugh had a rough edge that climbed inside her and fired her soul. "That is what I want . . . for now."

"And that is what I shall agree to."

"For now?"

She smiled. "For now."

He cradled her against him. Listening to his heartbeat, she let herself float along on its rhythm that matched the clip-clop of the horses' hooves on the cobbles. The carriage slowed to a stop, and she hid her dismay. She had hoped the ride would go on forever. As long as she rode in Galen's arms, she could pretend it could be like this all the time. Once again he was correct. She wanted to be with him.

The door opened, and Galen stepped out. He held up his hands. She put her fingers on one, then gasped when he swept his arms around her and lifted her off the seat.

"Galen, are you mad?"

"Probably." He cocked a single eyebrow in a clear challenge.

"You will hurt your side further with these antics."

"Probably." His voice was tight, and his smile evaporated.

"Then put me down."

"I think that would be wise."

Phoebe waited for him to move; then she realized that putting her down might hurt him worse. She shouted to Tate to come and help.

The door of Thistlewood Cottage swung wide, and Vogel rushed out to help. As the butler took Phoebe into his own arms, Galen leaned on Tate who helped him into the cottage. With the tact of a diplomat, the butler greeted them serenely. "Good evening, my lord, my lady. Lady Phoebe, your room is ready whenever you wish to retire."

Phoebe glanced at Galen who was struggling not to grin, even though his face was tight with pain. Because he knew that the butler was well aware where Galen had retrieved her from or because it was ridiculous to be talking to the butler while Vogel held her? Either way, she intended to put an end to this.

She tapped Vogel's arm. He set her on her feet, but his face remained as calm as if nothing had been out of the ordinary. She brushed her gown over her filthy shoes and realized she had left her parasol and bonnet at Miss Raymond's. Now she understood why Galen's lips were twitching. She must look like a complete hoyden after her misadventures.

"Thank you, Vogel," she said, deciding to follow the butler's lead and act as if nothing were out of the ordinary.

"You are welcome, my lady." He shifted with obvious disquiet before saying, "Mr. Townsend left a message for you, my lord."

"About what?" Galen winced again and put his hand to his left side.

"About his plans for this evening. Mr. Townsend asked that you—"

Phoebe interrupted, "Delivering that message will have to wait until Lord Townsend has had a chance to rest. Tate, take him into the parlor while I change. Vogel, Lord Townsend would like some brandy to ease his discomfort."

"You are a termagant tonight." Galen chuckled. "I suspect I would be a fool not to acquiesce to your orders."

"There would be no need for orders if you would not risk yourself with silly heroics."

He caught her arm as she was about to go to the steps leading to the wing where the bedchambers were. "Silly?" he asked, his voice a deep growl. "Was I an air-dreamer to believe that you might appreciate what I did for you this evening?"

"I meant only trying to sweep me off my feet and carry me into the cottage." She chose each word carefully, aware of Tate and Vogel, who were reluctant witnesses to this. "I appreciate everything else you did for me tonight."

"Everything?"

She smiled when the twinkle in his eyes warned that he was thinking more of the kisses they had shared than of how he had saved her reputation. Brushing her lips against his cheek, she whispered, "Everything." She laughed, then said, "Now go and sit and sip your brandy so you do not hurt yourself worse."

"Yes, my lady." He started to bow but paused.

"Vogel," she said, "please assist Lord Townsend to the parlor before his own skimble-skamble injures him."

The butler nodded, and she thought she saw his lips twitching. She hurried up the few steps toward her bedchamber. This had been a most extraordinary day, and she was glad it was over. She needed the night to think about what she would do now. She needed to go back to London, but she had promised Galen that he could escort her to a soirée. Her trip to Town must be postponed another day, and then . . .

For the first time in five years, she had been able to stop thinking about the rescues that had filled her life. Now, as she touched the jewelry box Galen had given her again, she wanted to think only of Galen and how his kisses sent a fiery rush of delight through her. She intended to savor them as long as she could, because she knew how short this delightful interlude would be.

Thirteen

Sipping on his brandy, Galen winced as each breath ached through him again. By Jove, it was so easy to forget this injury when he drew Phoebe into his arms. He wished it was as easy to forget her words.

He had been want-witted to try to play her dashing hero and carry her into the cottage like a knight of old rescuing his fair damsel by taking her over the drawbridge to safety. Her retort, based far more on reasonable behavior than his actions had been, had infuriated him for the moment before her next words made him see his lack of sense.

Phoebe was always so blasted sensible. Even her work to steal convicts from the ships was based on a peculiar logic that made sense when she explained it. At the very least, she should be pleased that, instead of going himself, he had sent Tate and the carriage to retrieve Carr who had sent word that his horse had gone lame on one of the roads beyond Bath. What his brother had been doing far from Bath all day was a question that could not be answered until Carr returned here.

"You are scowling. Are you in pain?" asked Phoebe as she walked into the parlor.

Galen hid his smile as he admired her loveliness,

now properly framed by neatly combed hair and a clean, pale green gown. He was tempted to tell her that he preferred her with her golden hair falling free and a spot of dirt on the tip of her upturned nose.

Quietly, he said, "If I tell you that I am indeed in pain, I collect you will chide me again for being less than sensible."

"Probably," she replied in the same terse tone he had used out by the carriage.

He laughed, then put his hand to his side. "I deserved that."

"But you did not deserve this pain." She knelt by his chair. "I owe you a debt I can never repay for all you have done for me."

"It has been my pleasure." He put his hand over hers on the chair. Gazing into eyes that glowed with pleasure at his touch, he wondered if any moment could be as perfect as this one.

The moment ended when Vogel came into the parlor. "Mr. Townsend to see you, my lord."

Galen pushed himself to his feet, ignoring the pinch along his side. Why was the butler announcing Carr as if his brother were a stranger?

"Get out of my way!" came a bellow from the hall.

"Oh, my," murmured Phoebe beside him as she rose with a whisper of silk.

Galen was tempted to repeat her words but was silent as his brother stormed into the room. Water splashed from every step Carr took, because he was drenched from head to foot. Glancing at the windows, Galen saw that it was not raining. What had soaked his brother? As Carr came closer, Galen's nose wrinkled. Whatever had washed over his brother, it was not rain.

When Phoebe choked, Galen pulled a handkerchief from beneath his coat. He handed it to her, wanting to apologize for the malodorous stench coming from his brother. She pressed the linen to her face, but not before he saw that the choking sound had not been coming from her attempt not to retch. She was trying not to laugh.

"By Jove, Carr, what happened to you?" he asked, steeling himself for the fury that was sure to spurt at him.

"I was attacked by two bumpkins." He touched his cheek that was obviously bruised. "They took offense for no reason at all."

"No reason at all?"

Carr tore off his coat and threw it on the floor. Vogel rushed to pick it up before the odor from it sank into the rug. Tugging off one boot, Carr flung it at the hearth. He pulled on the other boot, but it must have gotten stuck because he hopped about in a circle like a half-mad hare. Finally he got it off and sent it flying as he had the first.

Phoebe gave a soft cry when it hit a vase that wobbled and fell to the floor, shattering. "Have you lost what little sense you ever had?"

"Mayhap it was beat out of me," Carr fired back.

She started to reply, but Galen put his hand on her arm as he asked, "Why did they give you such a thrashing?"

"You would have known if you had been there."

"Excuse me?"

Carr strode toward them and jabbed a finger at the top button of his brother's waistcoat. "I sent you a message that my horse had gone lame and I needed a way home."

"I sent the carriage for you."

"Too late. I thought I could depend on you, Galen."

Phoebe could not remain silent any longer. "He did

the best he could to keep you from having to walk back to Thistlewood Cottage."

"I sent that message more than two hours ago," Carr said, not looking at her. All his fury was focused on his brother.

"I was not here when it arrived." Galen seated Phoebe on a settee and sat beside her. "As soon as I returned, I sent Tate to bring you home. Did he miss you along the road?"

"He met me on the bridge."

Galen nodded. "Then why are you complaining?"

"I could have been killed! You should have come to my assistance."

"I told you that I was not here when your message arrived."

Finally Carr looked at Phoebe. "And where were you?"

"I was retrieving Phoebe who had been calling on a friend of this family," Galen replied.

Carr snarled a curse that sent heat flashing up Phoebe's face but added nothing else as Mrs. Boyd came into the parlor.

The housekeeper's smile was strained, so she must have heard the raised voices from the hallway. Her voice had a brittle brightness. "I thought a light supper would be welcome, my lord."

Phoebe smiled. She had missed both her tea and supper, and cakes were set on one side of the tray. "Those look luscious."

With a laugh, Galen took one of the delicately frosted cakes as the housekeeper set the tray on a table in front of the settee. He handed it to her.

"Thank you," she said.

"You should have known that Sandra Raymond could not provide you with a meal at this time of day,"

Carr said as he reached in front of his brother and picked up a cup and the pitcher of cream.

Phoebe froze with the cake halfway to her lips. She quickly lowered it, her appetite gone.

"Miss Raymond?" asked Galen. "I do not recall saying where Phoebe was."

She wanted to congratulate him on his tone, which suggested he had no idea what his brother was talking about. Taking a small bite of the cake, she chewed it. The cake had a light lemon scent, but she could not taste it through her dismay.

"But you did say," Carr said. "You said she was at the house of a friend of the family. That Phoebe needed assistance to return here from making that call suggests that it was not a commonplace one. Putting that with the fact that Sandra is a very good friend of this family suggests you had to retrieve her from a most unexpected call." He gave his brother a superior smile. "The last time I spoke with Sandra, she asked where you were and why you had not called on her as you have before, Galen."

Phoebe submerged the gasp that threatened to betray her shock. She was not going to give Carr the satisfaction of viewing her dismay at his accurate guess. Or was it just a guess? Had he heard something that had revealed the truth?

"Odd," Galen said as he selected a cake for himself. As he sat back on the settee, his elbow jabbed Phoebe in the side.

She looked at him and saw his taut smile. Hoping she was saying the right thing to go along with whatever he planned to say, she asked, "What is odd?"

"Miss Raymond should know why I have not called on her." He faced his brother again. "I had no reason to visit her to save you from your own folly when you were involved in fisticuffs in daisyville."

"Until Phoebe gave her a look-in?"

Phoebe saw Carr watching her closely, so she gave him her most brilliant smile. "Miss Raymond," she said, keeping her voice light, although her heart ached, "was an excellent hostess when she invited me in to escape the storm."

"She does have *that* reputation." Carr laughed again.

"Carr, you should recall yourself." Galen set himself on his feet. "You are speaking to a lady, not one of your convenients. Phoebe is trying to be gracious about a most ungracious situation."

Laughing as she reached for a cup for herself, Phoebe said, "But Miss Raymond was also most gracious. She went out of her way to protect my reputation after she realized I was not interested in the opportunity to work for her."

Galen's laugh echoed off the ceiling, but she saw anger still darkened his eyes as he sat again. "Did you accept?"

"She intimated that she believed I could do quite well." Her smile became sincere. "I have never thought of myself as a businesswoman, so that was a compliment."

When Carr muttered something, she adroitly changed the subject. He said little at first, and she guessed he was vexed that she had not shattered into tears at his insinuations.

Trying to clear her mind, Phoebe leaned back in her chair as Galen talked to his brother about the gathering at the duchess's house the next night. She rocked her cup and watched the tea swirl within it. A hand over hers caused her to look up to see Galen smiling at her. With a smile of her own, she said, "I must own that it is good to be . . ."

"Home?" When she lowered her eyes, he reached to tip her face up toward him.

She drew back before Carr could make some sort of inflammatory comment. Coming to her feet, she said, "I bid you gentlemen a good evening. No doubt Carr wishes to get cleaned up from his adventures, and I believe I shall bring this exciting day to an end."

"Phoebe . . ." She was astonished when Galen came to his feet and faced her. She clasped her hands as her fragile smile vanished. How she longed to wrap her arms around him and delight in the rapture he offered.

"Shall we have a walk in the garden before retiring?" Galen asked.

"It is so late," she hedged. She fought her wayward heart, which urged her to forget the pangs of her conscience and take this chance to be with him . . . alone. "I have nothing to put over my shoulders."

"Both problems are easily solved, my dear," he said, holding out his hand. "You had a long nap this afternoon, so you cannot be tired." He strode to the bellpull. When Vogel appeared almost instantly, Galen added, "Please bring Lady Phoebe's paisley shawl."

Vogel nodded before going back out into the hall.

"How did you know I had a paisley shawl?" Phoebe asked.

"All ladies have a paisley shawl." Galen laughed heartily. He was facing her, so his brother could not see how he flinched with pain at the motion. "Carr, excuse us. I cannot resist discovering how the moon glistens off Phoebe's hair."

She used the same light tone he had, wondering if he had to strain to make it sound genuine as she did. "You are a charmer, Galen Townsend."

"I try, but you see through my ploys." He took her shawl from Vogel and placed it over her shoulders.

"Galen," Carr said as Galen led her toward the doors at the back of the room.

"Yes?"

Phoebe watched as Galen turned and the brothers locked gazes. If some unspoken message passed between them, she was not privy to it.

"I thought we were going to raise a cloud with some of those excellent cigars I brought from Town, Galen," Carr said.

"Damn," Galen muttered. "Too many people in this house."

"There are just the three of us," she said as softly.

"Which is one too many." He raised his voice so his brother could hear. "Even raising a cloud will not lessen the stench of your clothes, Carr. Why don't you clean yourself and we will light those cigars when I get back?"

Carr's scowl deepened, but he nodded.

Galen put his finger to his lips when she started to speak as they crossed the terrace toward the gardens that were sleeping in the shadows. She nodded, although she was unsure what he wanted to keep her from saying.

Looking at the city on either side of the river, Phoebe took a deep breath of the damp air, which was clean of odors. From the distance came the call of a watchman announcing all was well. The jangle of harness and the clang of horses' hooves rang clearly through the night.

He slipped his fingers through hers as they walked from the thick shadows beneath one tree to the next. She waited for him to speak, but he said nothing until they reached a bench set on a knoll overlooking the river. No houses blocked the view of the river and the Abbey beyond it.

"I like this spot," he whispered. "It reminds me of

a spot at Townsend Hall where Carr and I used to play when we were children. We would go there with our nurse and spend hours looking up at the star-strewn velvet of the night sky."

"My father often took me out to see the stars at Brackenton Park. He said there might come a time when I would need to find my way by following the stars." She shook her head. "How long ago that seems. I never would have imagined how my life would unfold."

"And that you would spend the afternoon in a brothel?"

She laughed. "That is not what I meant, but it is also quite true."

"What is it about you that urges me to share such silly, unimportant details of my childhood?"

She hesitated. To speak the truth of how she longed to be familiar with everything about him would mean owning—to herself and to him—that she was in love with him. "Mayhap because you want to think about when times were simple and all troubles could be healed with an extra dessert."

He leaned against the tree and crossed his arms on his chest. "As you do?"

"As I wish I could."

"If you believe that, then why are you so distrustful of everyone?"

With a sigh, she went to sit on the marble bench. When he sat beside her, she knew she must be honest. "I do not want to endanger anyone else in the life I have chosen."

"So you keep everyone far from you?"

"Yes."

Slipping his arm around her shoulder, he brought her back against him. Her head rested on his shoulder, and his mouth brushed against her ear, flinging a shiver of anticipation through her. "But, Phoebe, I do not want to be far from you. I would like to hold you very, very close."

Trying to sound as if she were joking, she asked, "Why should I give to you for free, Lord Townsend, what I was offered money for today?"

"You would never be a good harlot." His voice remained serious.

"And why not? Miss Raymond was anxious to hire me."

He stroked her cheek. "She saw only your beauty, which a man would pay high to possess. However, you could not hold yourself in abeyance as a harlot must."

"I don't understand."

"They sell only their bodies. When I hold you, you offer all of yourself. With you, there is no dividing line. You must give all or nothing." He hesitated, before adding quietly, "That is the same as you expect in return, isn't it?"

"Galen, I—"

"No, don't say it." Coming to his feet, he offered his hand. "I think we should return to the house."

"We cannot pretend this conversation did not happen. Or the conversation in the parlor never took place." She grasped his hand with both of hers. "Carr's discovery of where I was seemed to come too easily."

"I know. We have many friends in Bath, for our family has visited here often since we were children."

"So why did he guess I was at Miss Raymond's house?"

"That is something I need to discover for myself."

She shivered, although the night was still warm. "If he happened to see me go into the house, others may have as well."

"He must have been outside of Bath when you were caught in the storm."

"This makes no sense."

"I agree." He led her through the doors to the parlor, which was empty. Carr must still be ridding himself of his filthy clothes. "I intend to find out straightaway what he knows and how."

"And why."

"Why?" He faced her. "Yes, I need to know that as well. I expect he will tell me . . . eventually." Taking her hands, he folded them between his and pressed them over his heart. "Mayhap you will trust me eventually as well."

"I do trust you."

"You do?" His astonishment unsettled her even more.

Drawing her hands out of his, she whispered, "I trust you, but—"

"You don't trust yourself?" His smile became cool. "That is too pat an answer, I fear."

" 'Twas your answer. Not mine."

"And what is your answer, Phoebe?"

"I trust you," she said, knowing she must be honest as she had not in so long, "but I do not trust those who would wish to halt me from helping those I help. They would take any opportunity to destroy my allies along with me."

"You could have asked me if I was willing to take that risk."

"No, I could not." She stepped back from him, then leaned forward and steered his mouth to hers. This kiss, unlike the one in the garden, came from desperation. She wanted to savor this sweet rapture while she could. As his arms came up to enfold her, she edged away. "Good night, Galen."

"It could be, my dear."

For the length of a single heartbeat, she almost gave into the beseeching of her heart. Serendipity had brought Galen into her life, and she would be foolish to throw away this happiness he brought to her.

But she was a fool. She had owned to that the night she first went to the Pool and paid to have Jasper's brother freed from the ship sailing to Australia. When she rushed away out into the corridor, she heard the rattle of a glass decanter behind her in the parlor. Brandy might offer solace to Galen who had discovered she could never be his, but she had only her silly promise to help others to offer her comfort tonight.

It no longer was enough.

Fourteen

The house was quiet when Phoebe walked out of her bedchamber into the twilight-lit hallway. All day, she could have believed she was the only one in Thistlewood Cottage. Even Mrs. Boyd had been subdued, going about her chores without her normal cheerful singing and prattle.

Just as her house was on Grosvenor Square on the days after she returned from the Pool.

Why had she never noticed how disquieting this silence was? It crawled under her skin and sent a vexing pulse along her as if someone she could not see stood too close. She was aware of everything and everyone, but her thoughts wandered and she nearly walked into a footman who was carrying an armload of blankets from the laundry to the storage chests. Apologizing, she hurried toward the front door. Her fan, tied to her wrist with a bright blue ribbon, threatened to fly away on every step.

She could not escape the one thought that had haunted her all day. In the back of the cupboard in her bedchamber, her bag was packed with all she would need when she took the mail coach back to London tomorrow morning. The rest of her clothes would have to be returned later, because she could not pack them without revealing her plan.

Last night had forced her to make this decision she had wanted to postpone. In Galen's arms, she had been ready to set aside everything else to savor his touch. She could not while she was obligated to continue her work as Lady Midnight.

The note she had received this morning from her butler Johnson had been terse, but she had learned to read the meaning in the words that seemed so commonplace. Somehow, Jasper had found out where she was. That did not surprise her, because Jasper had ways of gaining information that amazed her. However, if her assistant could learn so quickly that she was here at Thistlewood Cottage, others might as well. Then her tale of coming down from London more than a week ago would fall apart and the truth might be revealed.

A ship was sailing out of the Pool at the beginning of next week. On it was scheduled to be a young woman who had been falsely accused of robbery by a lord when she had turned down his offer of becoming his mistress. The young woman was Jasper's brother's betrothed, and Jasper was desperate to rescue her.

Although her assistant would never ask her to risk herself for this woman, Phoebe must. Jasper could have been killed during their last visit to the docks. She owed him this duty, and she did not want to fail him.

After that . . . Phoebe faltered as she realized that she wanted to be done with this conspiracy. The recent days with Galen had revealed how she longed to reclaim her own life, which had been set aside after her father's death and the beginning of her rescue work.

All thoughts of her responsibilities vanished when

Phoebe saw Carr Townsend standing alone by the door in the foyer. Dash it! Why hadn't she paused to realize that he might be here before Galen was? Raising her chin, she kept her steps even as she crossed the foyer.

He took her hand and bowed over it. When he would have brought her fingers to his lips, she withdrew it not too gently. He frowned, but she did not let her expression waver as she stared at the ruddy mark on his cheek, his souvenir of the milling he had suffered last night.

"I see you are going to parade my grandmother's rubies at the duchess's assembly, so that everyone might know that Galen bestowed them upon you in return for whatever favors you have done for him."

"I have done him no favors. All the kindnesses have been from him."

Carr's smile was cold. "Yes, my brother does have a weakness for blondes. I should have known he would add you to his list of conquests."

"You are insulting!"

"To you or to my brother?" He laughed, but his eyes remained frigid. "Do you think a staid assembly this evening will entertain you after your exciting day yesterday?"

Phoebe knew she must not show him how much his cruel words hurt. Keeping her chin high, she said, "I am looking forward to the opportunity to speak further with the guests who called here two evenings ago."

"A very polite answer that does not answer my question."

"I thought it did. I am looking forward to seeing friends."

He rubbed his fingers against his chin. "Have you given thought to the idea that you may see others tonight whom you may not wish to see?"

"I never consider that when I prepare for a gathering." She looked past him. Where was Galen? It was not like him to be late.

"I would if I were you."

"You are not me." How much more bothersome could this man be? Galen could vex her with his questions, and he could entice her away from good sense with his delicious kisses, but he was nothing like his brother who seemed to talk in circles and say nothing and yet hope to send her up to the boughs.

"No, I was not chased by men through the streets of Bath yesterday."

Phoebe gasped and looked at Carr who was grinning broadly. "How do you know of that?"

"Know of what?" asked Galen as he stepped into the foyer. He adjusted his gloves, which were as white as his cravat and breeches. His black coat was still lighter than his ebony hair.

"We were speaking of her adventure yesterday," Carr replied, his smile now triumphant.

"I am sure," Galen said, "that Phoebe would rather speak of other things."

"Yes." She stepped forward. "I would like to speak of how you know what you do about—"

Carr turned away to look out the door. "Ah, here is my carriage." He walked out without adding anything else.

Phoebe clenched her hands on her fan until she heard the spines creak. She released it, not wanting to break her favorite fan. "Carr is not attending the assembly?"

"He wishes to be able to leave when he wants." Galen's lips grew straight. "And get himself into more of a muddle. He seems determined to get his daylights darkened here in Bath."

"He may get his wish. That bruise could become a black eye easily."

He took her hand and lifted it to his lips. She held her breath as she savored the incredible sensation of his mouth against her. His fingers ran along her cheek as he said, "You shall steal every man's eyes tonight, for they shall wish to follow you home."

"What a loathsome idea!"

"I did not intend it to be. Why, when I am with you, can't I think of the nothing-sayings that have served me so well in the past?"

"Mayhap because you want honesty from me, so you are honest yourself."

"Now that is, as my tie-mates would be quick to say, a loathsome idea. A lady is supposed to be lathered with court-promises and compliments, not the truth."

She put her hand on his proffered arm. "Who told you that?"

"I would suspect a lady."

As she walked with him out of the house to where Tate stood by the carriage, Phoebe laughed. She truly appreciated Galen's jesting, especially when she was so uneasy about this evening. She must not allow him to guess how she planned to sneak out of Thistlewood Cottage at dawn and go to the inn where the mail coach would be leaving for London, for he would be determined to halt her.

She looked out the window as the carriage turned onto the road leading into the center of Bath. When her hand was taken, she faced Galen.

"It will be fine," he said quietly.

"I hope you are right."

"On this, I believe I am."

She did not demur. "If rumors of what happened to me yesterday reach the *Beau Monde,* I will be ruined."

"And you will have no alibi for your work by the Pool?"

"Yes."

"That is more important to you than the damage to your family's name?"

Putting her other hand over the one holding hers, she said, "My parents raised me to do what I thought was right unless it brought harm to someone else. To bring shame on the Brackenton name would cause distress to my father's cousin who now holds the title. I would not wish that."

"I had not given that poor chap any thought." His smile became wry. "It seems, however, you have given great thought to every aspect of this obligation you have taken upon yourself."

"During the past five years, I have had many times to consider the consequences of my actions."

The carriage bounced in a chuckhole, and Galen grimaced as his head hit the roof. Rubbing the spot that had struck the roof, he said, "Yet I suspect you are considering the consequences of someone else's actions tonight."

"If Carr says anything to anyone—"

"He gave me his word that he will not." His smile became tight. "I know you find him irresponsible and not worthy of your trust, but he has never broken a promise to me."

Phoebe let her breath sift out in a sigh. "That is so good to know."

"But?"

"But?"

"I heard a 'but' in your voice."

Her fingers clenched in his hand. "If Carr knows where I was yesterday, someone else might as well."

"He and Sandra Raymond are very good friends."

"I suspect she has several *very good friends.*"

Galen leaned back and smiled. "She will lose those very good friends if she prattles one's business to another. That she spoke to Carr of this astonishes me, but she may have thought, since we are all staying at Thistlewood Cottage, he would be concerned by your disappearance."

"I hope that is all that it was."

"What else could it be?"

Phoebe had no answer for that. When Galen changed the subject to something he had read in the newspaper that had been delivered from London this afternoon, she tried to pay attention. It was impossible to shift her thoughts away from what might happen this evening.

Carr Townsend was a spoiled child who demanded every bit of his brother's attention. She could not say that *again* to Galen, who saw taking care of his brother as his duty. How could she tell him that his obligation was absurd when he could say the same back to her?

She watched Galen's face as he spoke, his expression emphasizing every word, and wished this interlude was not doomed to be so fleeting. There was so much she wanted to learn about this man whose kisses fascinated her and whose wit forced her to hone her own. The idea of flinging her arms around him and pressing her mouth to his was so tempting—but she must not. She might make him suspicious with her untoward behavior, and leaving on the morrow would be even more difficult.

"Ah, here we are," Galen said, drawing her attention back to his words instead of to her own unsteady thoughts. "Her Grace's house."

Phoebe looked out at the house that was set amidst a terraced row constructed of Bath stone, which glowed like tarnished gold in the light of the lamps hanging on either side of the door. Letting Galen hand her out, she was glad when he drew her hand into his arm and put his fingers over hers. He must be able to feel them tremble, but he said nothing as they walked up the pair of steps to the door and into the foyer.

The house was as grand as any on Berkeley Square. Gilt decorated the newel, which was carved to match plaster vines edging the ceiling. The silk wall covering was an icy blue barely warmed by the light from the huge chandelier that dropped from the roof four floors above.

Abruptly Phoebe tensed. The stiffening of her shoulders had become a habit since she had first come to Town in pursuit of one young man who had been wrongly accused. She was among friends who would be horrified if they ever guessed where she went when she excused herself from an assembly or a musicale.

A footman greeted her and Galen. They followed him up a curving staircase. Even before they had reached the top of the stairs, the sound of voices wove through the melodies of violins to welcome them into the ballroom.

Phoebe stared about the grand room. This ballroom was fancier than anything she had seen in London, because the carvings that decorated the ceiling were as intricate as the pattern woven into a rug. Two chandeliers, smaller versions of the grand one above the foyer, splashed their light over the plasterwork. The contrast of light and shadows created an ever-changing pattern as they entered the room.

She tore her gaze from the ceiling to see musicians set in an alcove high on the wall. No minstrels' gallery had ever been as elegantly painted with gold and rich blue. Beneath it, the guests mingled, sharing conversation and the wine that was being carried about the room by footmen.

"Lady Phoebe Brackenton, Your Grace," Galen said as he bowed over the duchess's time-wrinkled hand.

"We have met," the duchess replied and smiled at Phoebe. "At Almack's two years ago."

Phoebe searched her memory as she returned the white-haired woman's smile. The duchess was dressed in a gown as magnificent as her house and as brightly colored for it was an intense purple with a bright red sash decorated with all sorts of medallions.

Although Phoebe could not recall meeting the duchess, she said, "You are kind to remember me, Your Grace."

"It is easy when I remember meeting your father as a young man about your age. He had the same twinkle in his eye as this young man." She tapped Galen's arm with her closed fan. "I have heard very little about you recently, my boy."

"I had understood that you were residing full-time here in Bath," Galen replied.

"But that does not mean that I do not hear the news from Town. Are you still busy watching over your brother?"

"I find it far more delightful," he replied, "to watch over Lady Phoebe."

The duchess laughed. "You are always skilled with a *bon mot,* young man. Is young Carr with you?"

"He took a separate carriage."

"Then I shall expect to greet him soon." She tapped him on the arm again with her fan. "Go and get Lady Phoebe some of the champagne I thought would be the best way to begin our convivial evening. I trust you will return to speak to me at least once or twice before dinner."

"It will be my pleasure." He bowed his head again.

When the older woman gave him an enthusiastic hug, Phoebe saw him wince. One of the medallions must have been pressed against the spot where the knife had cut him.

The duchess must not have noticed because she said, "Bah, do not lather an old woman with false compliments. You would prefer to spend your time with this young lady." She leaned toward him and whispered something Phoebe could not hear.

Galen smiled as he drew Phoebe's hand within his arm again. Leading her toward the middle of the room, he shook his head when she started to ask what had been so amusing. Only when they were out of earshot of their hostess did he pause. He picked up two glasses from a golden tray held out by a footman.

Handing one to her, he said, "The duchess is renowned for her plainspeaking, so, no doubt, she feared she might offend you with her words."

"I do not offend easily. I have heard the basest of language in . . . London." She glanced about, hoping that if anyone was listening to their conversation, her hesitation would not be noted.

"No one is heeding us," Galen said. He touched his left side gingerly. "They are all too busy sharing the latest *on dits* from Town."

"Are you all right?"

"Still tender, and the duchess is as effusive as a doting grandmother."

She recognized that offhand tone. He did not want to discuss his injury. That was all for the good, because she had other questions for him. "Will you tell me what the duchess said?"

"Of course."

Phoebe waited, but he did not add more. Seeing how his eyes glistened, she asked, "Well?"

"It was little more than she congratulated me for choosing you as a companion rather than Carr."

"She is plainspeaking."

"As you would like to be."

She shook her head. "To the contrary, I find that words often provide the very shield one needs to hide the truth." She hesitated before going on. "You said it was little more than congratulations. What little more?"

"You are as curious as a kitten tonight, aren't you?" Laughing, he tapped his glass against hers.

Its single crystal note caught the attention of the other guests around them. Before Phoebe could ask another question, two men and a woman she did not know began to talk with Galen. He acted as if they were the best of friends, but she noted how he glanced at her as if gauging her reaction.

She wanted to accuse him of drawing them into others' conversations just when she was asking something he clearly did not intend to share. Galen had always been candid with her, hadn't he?

She no longer was certain, but she was sure that she was unsettled by the idea that this might not be the first secret he had kept from her. She had put her life and the lives of those she sought to help in Galen Townsend's hands. She even had dared to trust him with her heart. If he did not prove worthy of that trust, she might have traded everything she had worked to save for his kisses.

Fifteen

Mrs. Lyttle smiled as she looked across the crowded ballroom to where the duchess continued to welcome her guests. "I am so glad you and Lord Townsend accepted the duchess's invitation. I was saying to Mr. Lyttle just a few moments ago that it is pleasant to have new faces amid our small version of the Polite World in Bath."

"If one does not accept a duchess's invitation, one needs a very good reason," Phoebe replied with a laugh.

"You may not be surprised that Lord and Lady Windham sent their regrets for this evening's gathering, Lady Phoebe. *They* have a very good reason."

"I am sorry to hear that Lady Windham is not well, but I am happy for her and her husband." She tried not to look past Mrs. Lyttle to discover where Galen had gone. He had excused himself almost an hour ago. Nothing he had said when he took his leave had suggested that he would be gone this long.

"You are very kind."

"I could see they were very happy with the tidings." She kept her smile from faltering. Where was Galen?

"Are you having a pleasant visit here in Bath?"

"Yes, very." Would not Galen have told her if he had intended to take his leave of the duchess's party?

"I had expected to see you at the Pump Room yesterday," Mrs. Lyttle continued.

"I was quite busy yesterday. Mayhap on the morrow." Phoebe faltered. Lies were falling too readily from her lips. She would not be in Bath tomorrow if all went as she planned and she was able to take the mail coach to London.

When another woman began talking with Mrs. Lyttle about Lady Windham's delightful news of providing her husband with an heir, Phoebe excused herself. She wandered around the room, pausing only if no one seemed anxious to engage her in conversation. The whole of Bath must be crowded into this vast room that seemed so full. To find Galen amidst this assembly might be impossible.

The tenor of the conversation altered when the doors were opened and the guests were invited to dinner in another grand chamber, this one painted a vibrant crimson. Phoebe hung back as others poured through the doorway.

"Not hungry?" The mocking tone was too familiar.

She did not smile as she saw Carr's grin. The aroma of rum coming from him warned that he had been drinking something other than the duchess's wine. "Do not let me keep you from your meal," she said curtly.

"You shall not. I will enjoy everything that the duchess has to offer." He gestured to a maid. Smiling as he took a glass of wine from the tray she held out to him, he winked at the young woman. He tweaked her cheek and smiled more broadly as she rushed away, giggling.

When Carr arched a single brow at her, Phoebe did not retort. He was quite obviously determined to unsettle her. She wanted to tell him that he was too late. Galen's absence had upset her greatly already.

Carr's eyes slitted at the very moment a hand cupped her elbow. Her reaction rather than Carr's told her who stood behind her. Galen's casual touch flooded her with the longing to lean back and let his arms envelop her.

If Carr spoke before he stamped away with a frown, his words did not reach her ears, which were filled with the sound of her own racing pulse. She turned to Galen. When he held out his arm, she slowly slid her hand up his sleeve to the crook of his elbow. His smile widened in tempo with her touch. As his fingers swept along her cheek, he murmured her name.

Phoebe was tilting her mouth up for his kiss, but she froze when a jovial laugh from across the room struck her like a facer. How could she forget that so many people could be witnessing everything she and Galen did? Lowering her eyes, she asked herself how she could crave his caresses when she should be furious that he had left her with no explanation.

"Shall we join the others?" Galen asked, no emotion coloring his voice.

Phoebe met his gaze and saw the odd hollow expression in them. It was as if he had seen something that unnerved him to his very bones. Shuddering, she bit back all her questions as they went into the garish dining room, which must be as big as the one in the Royal Pavilion. Small tables were scattered around the room. As the other guests found their seats, she was relieved they were not sitting with Carr, who was wearing his most superior smile as he held court at the duchess's table.

Her relief became dismay when she realized she and Galen were sharing a table with the Lyttles. Being at a table with strangers would have allowed her to ask the questions that plagued her. However, she should be grateful. The Lyttles had a way of dominating all conversation, so there would be no chance for her to betray her plans for the morrow.

Galen seated her and spoke a greeting to the Lyttles. As he discussed with them the gossip that had been shared throughout the evening, Phoebe simply smiled. She could keep that expression on her face as long as she said nothing.

When the duchess came to the table to speak with Mr. Lyttle about the games of chance she wished her guests to play later in the evening, Phoebe asked softly, "What is bothering you, Galen? You look as if your thoughts are thousands of miles away."

" 'Tis better that mine are far away rather than yours are focused on issues that lead thousands of miles away."

She put her hand over his. "I am not jesting, Galen. You vanished, and then you reappeared. What is amiss?"

Galen was astonished anew how easily Phoebe read every nuance of his emotions. He wished he could do the same with her, but she had become so accustomed to deception that she guarded every expression and word. Yet she was the most honest woman he had ever met. Even the duchess with her outspoken ways still played the coquette. Phoebe was straightforward on everything, save for her midnight adventures.

He said nothing as bowls of steaming vegetable soup were placed in front of them. He lifted his spoon before he replied, "I would like to tell you that everything is perfect."

"I would like to hear you say that."

He leaned toward her. "Would you like to hear me say that everything is perfect as long as you are here with me? That nothing can be wrong when we are together?"

She smiled. "As I told you before, you are wasting your nothing-sayings on me, Galen."

"I would not say so."

When she looked quickly away, he was astonished to see a gentle flush climbing her cheeks. Pleasure? Or could it be amazement at his words? Why was she surprised? How could she not know how much he wanted her?

"Do not be sad." She placed her fingers lightly on his sleeve. "I could not tolerate it if you were sad tonight." Again she looked away.

He tipped her face back toward him and saw the longing in her eyes. Craving to hold her pierced him more fiercely than any weapon. "I have to own that I cannot be sad in your company."

"Odd that you say that, for you have seemed vexed more than once in my company."

He touched her cheek lightly, fighting his yearning to run his fingers along it. "Being vexed is quite different than being sad."

"Where did you go?" she asked.

"To get Carr."

"Oh, I see."

By Jove, that was not the reaction he had expected. He had thought she would be exasperated that he had brought her here, then gone to find out what was delaying Carr. Now he was the one who should *not* be surprised, he told himself. From the beginning, she had known that Carr found himself in trouble far too often.

"Townsend," said Lyttle, saving Galen from having to answer Phoebe, "if I may say so, you are an odd suitor."

"Excuse me?"

"Mr. Lyttle," chided his wife, "you should not tease Lord Townsend like that."

"Not tease him how, Mrs. Lyttle?"

"On how he courts Lady Phoebe, Mr. Lyttle."

"I meant only, Mrs. Lyttle, that when I was a young man with my eye set on a pretty lass, I would not have left her to wander about the ballroom alone."

Mrs. Lyttle wagged her finger at her husband. "You should not say such things when Lady Phoebe is here to hear them."

"Mrs. Lyttle, you should not scold me before the rest of gathering," Mr. Lyttle said.

"I am trying only to bring a smile to these two young people, Mrs. Lyttle."

"They might smile if they had a chance to speak, Mr. Lyttle."

Phoebe could not keep from smiling. She had become so immersed in all the trouble stalking her that she had forgotten why she liked spending time with the Lyttles. These little brangles were as entertaining for their friends as they were for the couple who had been married almost ten years.

When Galen choked back a laugh, she bent to take a sip of her soup before her own laugh burst forth. She put down her spoon as the conversation continued on the other side of the table. If the food was delicious or made of the coarsest sawdust, she could not tell, for everything was tasteless while she saw that shadow of sorrow in Galen's eyes. Even the dessert had no flavor. She noticed that Galen was not eating either. He toyed with his fruit and cake as she realized she was doing with the ruby necklace.

"Good evening, Townsend, Lyttle, ladies."

A dark-haired stranger stood behind Galen's chair. The man was dressed in an eye-blurringly brilliant blue waistcoat over pale breeches. His dark green cravat was fastened with a tastelessly large gold and diamond stickpin.

Galen's face contorted with disgust as he stood. When he spoke, she was sure she had never heard such loathing in his voice. "What are you doing here, Hill? I thought the duchess had better sense than to open her door to a blackguard like you!"

"I am welcome here among the Polite World in Bath, even though I did not inherit a fortune and a title."

"No, you chose to make your money in the trade of flesh!"

"As you well know, the trade in slaves is now illegal, thanks to shortsighted fools like your father."

Galen smiled. "Yes, thanks to men of good conscience like my father." His smile remained, but his face hardened. "I doubt if something as simple as a law has stopped your trips to Africa and the Indies for slaves."

Captain Hill placed his hand on the back of Phoebe's chair. When she drew away from his fingers, horrified that he might be involved in ripping people from their homes and families forever, she put her hand on her stomach. She did not want to be ill during the duchess's soiree, but she was sickened by the idea that Captain Hill was perpetrating a crime more appalling than sending people to Botany Bay for stealing a few shillings. She hoped Galen would find a way to end this conversation without delay.

Her hopes were for naught, she realized, when Captain Hill chuckled. "Now, Townsend, you know my ship's manifest has never been questioned."

"No?" Galen retorted with an icy laugh. "Is your memory as dull as your wit, Hill?"

"Never, I should have said, except for that one unfortunate incident you witnessed in London." His fury was revealed by his too-tight smile. "Of course, you know all the details of that. One of your cronies confiscated my cargo. No loss. Profits are higher than ever."

"Your cronies?" asked Phoebe before she could halt herself. She had not guessed that Galen had any connections on the docks of London. That he was familiar with ships and their captains was unsettling because he had not mentioned that.

Galen put his hand over hers. "Do not waste your attentions on this conveyancer."

Captain Hill smiled as he picked up her other hand and bowed over it. "Enough of this talk of business, Townsend. Aren't you going to introduce me to your lovely lady?"

"Lady Phoebe Brackenton," Galen said as he drew her hand out of Captain Hill's, "this poor excuse for a human being is Captain Paul Hill, smuggler and slaver. Watch that he does not relieve you of your baubles even as we speak. Good evening, Hill." He turned his back on Captain Hill and asked, "Would you help me put an end to this, Phoebe, by standing up with me?"

Captain Hill scowled. His thatch of black hair matched the dark emotions in his squinting eyes. As she came to her feet, she tried to avoid his sleeve. Despite his expensive clothes, he could not shake the stench of his ship. She glanced at Mr. Lyttle who also had come to his feet as she did. He had edged to stand between his wife and Captain Hill, telling her that Galen's abhorrence of this man was shared by Mr. Lyttle.

When Galen led her back through the doorway to the ballroom where the musicians continued to play, Phoebe knew Captain Hill was staring at them. She looked back and shuddered. Captain Hill was staring at *her*. A flush burned on her cheeks.

"Pay him no mind," Galen murmured.

"How can I pay him no mind when he is standing in the doorway and watching us?"

He drew her across the floor, letting other couples block them from Captain Hill's gaze. "I am sorry, Phoebe. I had not guessed that *he* would be here."

"He keeps staring."

"Do not look at him." His finger tipped her chin back toward him. "He is simply envious of me tonight."

"I doubt if Captain Hill feels anything as tepid as envy."

"You are worrying about something that does not matter."

She could not keep from looking back at the doorway. "If he sails into the Pool, do you think it is possible that he might recognize . . . that is . . . ?"

Galen's chuckle was cool. "I thought it would be wise not to give him time to consider the possibility that he might have seen you previously." He drew her into his arms and whirled her about the floor to the melody of the waltz. He lowered his voice as he bent toward her as if to whisper court-promises in her ear. "How often did you encounter the masters of the ships you harvested?"

"Never."

"Then you are fearing him for no reason. After all, he does not sail any farther than America."

She smiled. "Thank you for reminding me of that."

"Should I thank you as well for reminding me how much I delight in holding you close?"

"You are welcome, but I must own I don't forget that." Her fingers slipped up through his hair. "Galen, be honest with me."

"About Carr?"

"Yes." She wanted to add *among other things,* but it might be simpler to deal with one crisis at a time. She had to take care how she asked him about his connections to the ships that sailed from the Pool. He was her best ally now, and she must not insult him with demands that he explain why he never mentioned those connections before.

"I thought he should be reminded that he would be unwise to forget how much the duchess wished to speak with him."

"She seems quite fond of him."

"Her son attended school with Carr, so she has known him since he was a lad." He chuckled. "She has told me more than once how much Carr reminds her of her own son and heir. From the tales I have heard, I would say her estimation was quite accurate."

"And she seems quite fond of you."

"Now that I am thinking about it, I do believe she is the lady who told me that I could not make a mistake by filling a lady's ear with court-promises." He drew her even closer.

She wanted to rest her head against his shoulder and let the music swirl them into enchantment. Even though her heart pleaded with her to forget everything but this moment of delight, she had to know the truth.

"Galen, your comments to Captain Hill suggest that you are very familiar with ships and their captains," she said.

"The Townsend family has some interest in shipping. We are investors in several lines."

She pulled back to stare at him. "You never mentioned that before."

"It did not seem relevant."

"Relevant?" She lowered her voice when some of the other dancers stared at her.

Galen pulled her back into his arms and into the pattern of the waltz. "Phoebe, I have not lied to you, if that is what you fear."

"It is." She could not lie to him about this. She would save her lies for other things, such as not telling him about the note she would leave behind when she went to catch the mail coach.

"I have spoken with many of the masters of the ships in the Pool, but mostly when I have seen them in the taverns where Carr makes a sport of pursuing the serving wenches."

"Captain Hill spoke as if you have had a long acquaintance."

"He is a distant cousin of a friend from school, so I saw him occasionally on holidays." Galen smiled wryly. "Hill was obnoxious even then." He put his mouth close to her ear. "I do not wish to speak of that cur when I would rather relish this moment of holding you."

Phoebe agreed wholeheartedly with that, even as her heart threatened to shatter. She wanted to savor this precious moment of dancing with him because she knew how unlikely it was that she would ever savor it again. When she left Thistlewood Cottage without warning, she wondered if Galen would ever be able to forgive her.

She knew she would never be able to forgive herself for risking this chance for love.

Sixteen

"They make quite the couple, don't they?" Phoebe asked with a laugh as she watched Galen twirl the duchess carefully about the floor.

Mrs. Lyttle chuckled. "Her Grace seems to have never gotten over her youthful attraction to handsome men." Lowering her voice, she added, "I doubt if any woman has ever grown immune to a good-looking man. Her Grace simply has decided not to keep her admiration secret."

"What are two such lovely ladies doing here alone?" asked a deeper voice.

Phoebe tensed when she looked up at Captain Hill. "We are not alone, Captain. We are having a conversation with each other."

His eyes widened at her sharp reply, but he said, "Then I hope you will forgive this intrusion when I ask if you would dance with me, my lady."

"Phoebe, you need not stand up with him," Mrs. Lyttle whispered frantically.

She patted Mrs. Lyttle's hand, but her words were for Captain Hill, "Thank you for your offer, but I am enjoying my conversation here."

"Allow me to join in," he said, drawing a chair forward to face them.

"It is not a topic you would find interesting."

"Then allow me to speak of something we all should find intriguing."

Mrs. Lyttle sniffed. "You have nothing to say that I would find the least bit interesting, Captain."

"Quite to the contrary." His dark eyes glittered with amusement. "You cannot be the only ones uninterested in one of the most oft-repeated rumors tonight."

"I do not listen to gossip," Phoebe said. She wanted to motion for Mrs. Lyttle to get up, so they could both walk away. However, Captain Hill's chair blocked their way.

"Certainly you have heard what is being said about this traitor who is abducting low criminals off the ships that were meant to take them from London to where they will not be a burden upon us for the length of their transportation."

Phoebe snapped her fan open, hoping the motion would hide her sudden dismay. She had not guessed that anyone was speaking of *that* tonight. Knowing she must say something, she replied, "I did hear something about that earlier, but I paid it little attention." She wafted her fan in front of her, hoping no hint of blush would betray her. "I came to Bath to escape the problems of London."

"But this tale of what has happened at the Pool is so interesting." Captain Hill offered Mrs. Lyttle a smile. "I know you think so, Mrs. Lyttle, for I heard you speak to your husband's friends about this very subject."

"It is intriguing, if it is true." Mrs. Lyttle could not hide her regret that she had to agree with the mannerless man. "I do not know why any chap would risk his own neck for convicts."

Captain Hill chuckled. "Along the wharves near the Pool, it is whispered that this Robin Hood–type creature is in truth a woman. She is called Lady Midnight, because she comes with the darkness and is never seen."

"I have heard that name repeated over and over, but I do not believe this person who is being sought by the authorities is a woman," Mrs. Lyttle said coolly. "No lady with even the least bit of wit about her would be found by the docks in the middle of the night. It would ring the death knell for her reputation."

"An interesting insight." Captain Hill turned to Phoebe. "And do you agree, my lady?"

She folded her hands in her lap and pasted her most simpering smile on her face. If he thought to trip her up with such a question, he was mistaken. She had learned to handle this sort of confrontation early on in her work.

"I have heard other tales of incredible beings," she said, borrowing Mrs. Lyttle's chilly tone. "Incredible creatures that sailors have invented to pass the time and whose exploits are magnified by the amount of rum in a bottle. This Lady Midnight sounds as if she belongs with stories of mermaids and great cities lost beneath the waves." She did not pause before adding, "Mrs. Lyttle, I believe that I see Lady Notell waving to us. Excuse us, Captain Hill."

Coming to her feet, Phoebe grasped Mrs. Lyttle's hand. Captain Hill backpedaled so they did not run him down. Hurrying Mrs. Lyttle across the room at the best pace the shorter woman's legs could manage, Phoebe only slowed when they were in the opposite corner.

"Lady Notell?" asked Mrs. Lyttle rather breathlessly. "I must own that I do not know this lady."

"Because she does not exist." Phoebe laughed. "I fear I told a complete banger to get us away from that scurvy pirate."

Mrs. Lyttle put her hand over her mouth, but her laugh bubbled out. "My lady, you betwattled him completely."

"I trust you will forgive me for making you a party to my falsehood."

"Anything to escape that—What did you call him?"

"Scurvy pirate." Phoebe laughed, too.

"Such language!" Carr stopped in front of them. "I did not expect to hear such from your lips, Phoebe."

"No?" She had not guessed anyone could make her regret leaving the conversation with Captain Hill, but it was just possible that Carr Townsend might. "I shall struggle to be more courteous in my descriptions from this point forward."

"You would not be discourteous enough to deny me the chance to dance with you, would you?"

She snapped her fan open as she had when speaking with Captain Hill. "You have a most peculiar way of asking a woman to stand up with you, Mr. Townsend."

"I await your answer."

Phoebe was about to tell him that she would not dance with him if he were the last man in England, then noticed Captain Hill coming toward them once more. Her heart thudded in fear against her chest. Even Carr Townsend was preferable to that mannerless lout who might find a way to discover the truth she hid.

Holding out her hand, she said, "My answer is yes, I will dance with you, Mr. Townsend. If you will excuse me, Mrs. Lyttle . . ."

"That old tough is going to swoon," Carr said with an icy laugh as he led her out to the middle of the room where the revelers were gathering for the next dance. "She does not speak kindly to me."

"Nor you to her, I would collect, for you have not guarded your language in my presence."

"You do have a serpent's tongue." He clamped his hand over hers on his sleeve. "It amazes me that Galen has endured it this long. Although I must own, he may find its other uses worthwhile."

"By all that's blue, I have never met a man in the Polite World who is so common in his manners." Phoebe stopped, then gasped as he pulled her forward a pair of steps. She looked around the room and saw Galen talking with Mrs. Lyttle. Mrs. Lyttle's hands waved to emphasize her words, and Phoebe saw Galen glance at where Captain Hill now stood by the back wall.

"And what do you think of the manners of those beyond the *ton?*"

"I have never met another with such low manners there either."

He laughed and drew her to one side of the room. By the wall, he seated her. She started to rise, but his heavy hand on her shoulder kept her on the chair.

"If you do not care to dance," she said primly, "I must ask you to excuse me."

"Not before you answer a few questions."

She clasped her hands in her lap and met his mocking gaze steadily. "I will answer your questions if you will refrain from acting like a vulgar cad."

"You do not mince words, I see."

"I find they taste better in my mouth when I speak with honesty."

"Then I shall be as candid. I know where my brother was when you met."

"As I do."

"I would wonder why a lady such as yourself would be found near that low place."

"Low?" She gave him a scowl that had daunted

others, save for Galen. "I believe the duke would be quite offended to hear you speak so of his lovely home."

"Duke?"

"I was attending His Grace's musicale when I first spoke with your brother." She came to her feet and continued to glare at him. When his eyes lowered, she almost smiled. This frown seemed as effective against his blustering as it had been with others. "I do not know what tales you have been listening to, Mr. Townsend, but you need only ask Lady Casterly, for she was in attendance that evening also."

He slowly raised his gaze up to meet hers. Amusement filled his eyes as well as fury. She had been foolish to think she could daunt him with a single glance. "You are glib, my lady. However, you know as well as I that I did not speak of that night, but of one a fortnight later. The night you left London."

"Then you should say what you mean." She turned to walk away, but again he put his hand on her shoulder.

Prowling around her, like a cat circling a broken-winged bird, he murmured, "You and Galen may think I am easy to bamboozle, but I know that he was bound for the Little Lost Lamb in search of me."

"And would he have found you there?"

"You are trying to change the subject, my lady."

She shook her head but did not look away. She wanted to see if Galen was through talking with Mrs. Lyttle, but she did not dare. Lowering her guard even for a moment with his brother could mean her doom. "Quite to the contrary," she replied. "I know how Galen worries about your thoughtless actions that are bound to lead you to ruin."

"But he did not wait to see if I had ruined myself

utterly that evening because he went with you to Thistlewood Cottage."

"Yes, he was kind enough one evening to offer me an escort to a friend's house when my own carriage was stolen."

"Near the Little Lost Lamb?"

Galen's laugh prevented her from having to devise a lie. Clapping his brother on the shoulder, he asked, "What would Phoebe be doing in that disgusting place? Her pursuits center on Mayfair, Carr, and now in Bath."

"I find it odd, brother, that you were to meet me at the Little Lost Lamb at the same time *on dits* suggest you were already in residence at Thistlewood Cottage."

"You should know by now that rumor has a way of baffling everyone," Galen replied. "A good use for rumor, I would say."

"I do not believe gossip has any good uses." Phoebe waved her fan in front of her face.

Galen smiled, wondering if she realized that her agitation was visible in her motions. In some ways, lovely Phoebe Brackenton was still quite unsophisticated. She was a peculiar mixture of strength and softness, pride and naïveté. In his arms, she offered an enticing promise. Her tentative touch against his chest told him that, despite her incredible beauty, she had no suspicions of the course of his thoughts when he held her in his arms. With her head on his shoulder, she could have been a child seeking consolation.

But she was no child.

Something that Hill had apparently taken note of, according to Mrs. Lyttle who had been distressed by the ill-mannered man asking Phoebe to dance.

"Excuse us, Carr," Galen said. "Phoebe promised

me another dance when I was finished dancing with
our hostess."

Carr scowled. "This evening is an utter bore."

"There are cards, if you wish to play."

"Even cards fill me with ennui. I shall have to find
something else to entertain me."

"Miss Parkman is in need of a partner for this
dance," Phoebe said.

Carr grumbled something under his breath, but
Galen paid him no mind as he steered Phoebe back
out to where another waltz was beginning. The duchess was making certain that everyone had a chance to
dance intimately this evening.

"Thank you," Phoebe whispered with relief.

Drawing her into his arms, he began to turn her to
the music. "For asking you to dance?"

"Of course not."

"You did not want to dance with me?"

When she smiled, he delighted in the joy rushing
through him like a springtide. This warmth on her face
lit his fantasies when he could not sleep, too over-
whelmed by his longing to hold her.

"You know," she said, her soft voice like a caress,
"I want to dance with you. What I intended to say
was that I am grateful for you intruding on my conversation with Carr. I was not sure if I could halt all
his questions."

"Do not think of them now. Think of dancing here."

She laughed as he swirled her through that dance
and the next. Knowing he should be a gentleman and
ask other women among the duchess's guests to dance,
he did not. He wanted to hold Phoebe and have the
wisps of her hair brush his face and breathe in her
sweet scent. As his fingers stroked her back, she gazed
up at him with the enticing smile that made him ache
to press his mouth to hers.

More than once, Galen noted Hill watching them. The blackguard even approached them once as a dance was ending. Stepping to where a quadrille was about to begin, Galen hoped Hill realized that Phoebe would not have the slaver's company inflicted upon her again this evening.

"You are going to have me dance my feet right through my slippers," Phoebe said when the orchestra took a recess for a few minutes.

"That sounds like regret."

She laughed again. "I have fancied every moment we have danced."

"Shall we sit until the orchestra returns?"

"Yes."

When he turned her toward chairs along the wall, she stiffened. He was not surprised to see Hill there. She abruptly grasped his hand and drew him into an alcove on the opposite wall from the minstrels' gallery.

"This is cozy," he said as he looked around the space where the only furniture was a crimson bench that matched the curve of the walls.

"It is quiet, but we can see if anyone is lingering near the open door."

He took two glasses from a passing servant. Handing her one, he said, "You are a master at deception."

"I have learned." Phoebe faltered, then, sitting, took a sip of wine before saying, "Just as your brother wishes to learn, Galen. He has been very focused on finding out the truth of what happened the night you were looking for him by the Little Lost Lamb."

"He is simply irritated that he had to find his own way home that night."

"Did he?"

He tipped her face back so he could see it. "Why are you questioning me on this?"

"Because I suspect you had your coachee send a

message back to Town to have your brother retrieved from whatever place he had taken himself to that night." She drew away from him. *"That* was the reason we stopped at the inn as soon as we had gone a few miles beyond London."

"How long have you suspected this?"

"Since the beginning, for I would have done much the same."

"So why are you speaking of it only now?"

She wrapped her arms around herself, although she wished he would wrap his around her. "I am very uneasy. Captain Hill—"

"Do not let that cur's boorish ways bother you."

" 'Tis not his ways, but what he has said." She lowered her voice. "He spoke of stories along the wharves in London of Lady Midnight."

"Which we have already heard."

"But he said others were speaking of it here tonight."

Galen chuckled and raised his glass. "Then allow me to offer a toast to this legendary lady whose escapades have set so many tongues to wagging."

"This is not funny. Just as it is not funny that you may have jeopardized everything because you insist on acting as a parent for your wastrel brother."

"Wastrel?"

Phoebe wanted to take back the heartless word, not because it was a lie, but because it had hurt Galen. When she started to speak, he waved her to silence.

"I have asked you to be honest with me," he said. "It is clear what your opinion of Carr is."

"He is using you, Galen."

"No, he simply needs my help, and, as his older brother, it is my place to offer it. Would you do any less?"

Phoebe wanted to give him a quick answer, but she

could not. Slowly shaking her head, she stared down at her wine. How could she be speaking so when she could not forget the packed bag at the back of her armoire? Her obligations were going to rip them apart more completely than any of Carr's childish antics.

As he offered his arm to bring her back out into the ballroom, she wanted to ask him to remain with her while they soothed the anger between them.

The duchess peered around the edge of the alcove. "Here you are! I have been looking all over for you, my boy."

"What is it?" Galen's face grew rigid. "You look distressed, Your Grace."

"That boy always distresses me."

"Boy?"

"Your brother, my boy. This was delivered for you." The duchess thrust a piece of paper into his hand.

Galen opened it, then smiled it at the duchess. "It is nothing out of the ordinary."

"I am glad. I— Oh, pardon me." The duchess scurried away at a pace usually unseen in a woman of her years. Her greeting to a friend reached into the alcove.

Phoebe ignored the duchess's voice as she watched Galen crumple the page into a ball. "Nothing out of the ordinary?" she asked. "More trouble?"

"Carr seems to find it wherever he goes."

"Where is he?"

"He has vowed, according to this note that his coachee passed to Tate, to repay those bumpkins who gave him a thrashing last night." He grimaced. "You may be quite right about my brother. He seems in need of a guardian to get him out of this pickle."

"Galen, I am sorry. If you must go and find out what Carr is up to, go."

"To assuage your conscience?"

She shook her head as she put her hands on his

arms. "No, you should go to ease yours. You have taken on this obligation, and I was wrong to belittle it. You have understood why I must do what I do."

"No, I do not understand that at all. I don't *want* to understand it. I want you to stop."

"I can't."

"You must."

Her eyes narrowed. "You sound as if I have a choice."

"You have a choice. You could stop any time you wished."

"I vowed to help these people."

"And you have."

Phoebe knew she must put an end to this conversation before she said the very worst thing: telling him that she intended to return to London posthaste. "Go," she urged. "Go and save your brother from his own carelessness."

"Only if you promise me that we will continue this conversation after I have retrieved him."

"Galen—"

"Promise me."

"I promise," she whispered, knowing that if she delayed Galen further, he might not return home before the mail coach was due to depart on the morrow.

He pulled her into his arms. "I may not be able to save him from his folly, but I must save you from yours."

His lips slanting across hers gave her no chance to reply. Not that she wanted to when she feared he would discover that she was kissing him good-bye.

There should have been a path cut into the rug.

As Phoebe paced between the window and the door to the hallway in the parlor of Thistlewood Cottage, she was sure she must be wearing out both her slippers and the pattern on the rug. She had not been surprised that Galen had not returned before she went to sleep. When neither he nor Carr had made an appearance when she woke, she had begun to worry.

At dawn, she had begun pacing. Now that midday had passed, along with the time when she should have left to get on the mail coach, she continued walking back and forth.

"Would you like some hot chocolate now, my lady?" asked Mrs. Boyd as she came into the parlor.

"I am not hungry."

"You must eat something, my lady."

Phoebe wandered from the center of the room back toward the window. "Mayhap later."

"Not eating will do nothing to bring Lord Townsend home." She wiped her hands on her apron. "Eating will allow you to be strong enough to help him when he arrives."

"Help him?"

"I should not have said that."

"But you did." Phoebe lowered herself onto the closest chair and motioned for Mrs. Boyd to take the one beside her. "I have seen your dedication to Lord Townsend. You would not have said that if you did not wish me to know it."

Mrs. Boyd sat on the chair, her hands folded in her lap. "I know you care for Lord Townsend, my lady."

"We have had this discussion before."

"Yes, that is why you should know that he is not a foolish man. He will do what he thinks is best for those he cares about."

"He has rescued Carr so often."

"So often that Mr. Townsend expects that he will continue to do so."

"Yes," Phoebe said. If she expressed her dismay

with that thought, she might offend Mrs. Boyd who had so much affection for Galen's family.

A throat was cleared, and Phoebe looked toward the doorway. Vogel was standing there, his hands clasped behind his back.

"Yes?" Phoebe repeated, but this time as a question.

"A Mrs. Gerber to see you, my lady."

"Mrs. Gerber? I don't know anyone by that name."

Vogel said, "She insists on seeing you, my lady. She says it is an emergency and that Jasper sent her."

"Jasper?" Phoebe came to her feet. "Bring her in without delay. Mrs. Boyd, thank you."

"Y-y-yes, my lady," Mrs. Boyd said, clearly shocked at the sudden dismissal. The housekeeper glanced at her again and again as she went out of the room.

Phoebe's fingers curled into fists. Later, she would apologize to Mrs. Boyd, even though the apology must be laced with lies. She could not trust anyone here . . . except Galen.

Why had Jasper sent someone to call on her here? Jasper should not have allowed even his name to be spoken here.

Vogel brought a woman to the door, then stepped away. Her simple dress was pocked with the same dust that had stolen the shine from her light brown hair. She must have been traveling for a long time. All the way from London? Or had she come from somewhere else? It did not matter. All that mattered was how this woman had come here with Jasper's name on her lips.

"My lady, thank you for seeing me," the woman said, staring at the floor.

"What can I do for you?" Phoebe asked the question with caution. Even at this juncture, she must be careful not to say anything to betray herself.

"You helped my husband, Charlie, my lady." She knelt and held up her hands. "Please help me now."

Phoebe took the woman's hands. Bringing her to her feet, she said, "Tell me your name."

"Mona—Mona Gerber."

"Mrs. Gerber, I do not know any Charlie Gerber."

"But you do. You helped him get off *The Southern Cross* before he could be sent to Botany Bay almost two years ago. You—"

"No, you are mistaken." Jumping to her feet, Phoebe rushed to the door. She looked around and saw no one. She hoped no one stood just out of sight. Mrs. Gerber's words might carry through the house. Closing the door, she turned to face Mrs. Gerber. "Please sit," she said.

"Oh, Lor', my lady. I couldn't sit on that fine chair. I'll get it all dirty."

"Please sit." Her voice cracked as she whispered, "Please."

Mrs. Gerber sat, wide-eyed, while she stared at everything in the room. But when Phoebe took a seat across from her, Mrs. Gerber's eyes focused directly on her.

"You know that I should not be receiving you," Phoebe said.

"I know." She wrung a handkerchief with torn lace, then dropped it into her lap.

"How did you know where to find me?"

"That was easy. We all know where to find you." She smiled broadly. "Those of us who know we can depend on you, my lady, know that you left London and came here."

"Those of us?" She pressed her hand over her heart, which seemed to have forgotten how to beat. "Who?"

"Those of us who need you know where you are all the time." Mrs. Gerber smiled hesitantly, and Phoebe realized the woman was younger than she appeared. "We don't tell no one else. We know you have helped us, and we do not want to betray you."

"But you are here."

"I must see my Charlie."

"But if I were to help you, then others might come."

"That is true."

"You must see why I must say—"

Mrs. Gerber slipped out of the chair and knelt beside Phoebe again. "My lady, do not say no. Charlie's mother is dying. She wishes to see her son just once more."

Closing her eyes, Phoebe shook her head. "Anything I say will sound coldhearted."

"I am not asking for Charlie to come home. I simply am asking if he might see his mother one last time." Tears ran down Mrs. Gerber's face so fast she could not wipe them away. "He can be snuck in and out of the house without anyone being the wiser. I know he can, my lady. Then he can go back to wherever he has been since you took him off *The Southern Cross,* and he will finish his time."

"I must think about this."

"Please help us, my lady."

Phoebe took a deep breath. "I must think about this. Where can I reach you to let you know my decision?"

When Mrs. Gerber gave a street address at the far edge of Bath, Phoebe struggled to breathe evenly. Discovering that Phoebe was staying at Thistlewood Cottage must have been a temptation Mrs. Gerber could not ignore.

"I will be in touch as soon as I can," Phoebe promised.

Mrs. Gerber smiled so broadly that Phoebe was unsure how her smile could be held by her thin face.

As soon as the woman had taken her leave, Phoebe

sent Vogel to bring Tate to the parlor. The coachman had brought her home last night, because Galen had sent the coach back for her after he had collected his horse from the stable here. Although Tate was curious, he only nodded when Phoebe gave him instructions.

She went to the window to watch him walk toward Bath. He should not be gone more than an hour. By the time he arrived back with his information, Galen might have returned. Then she could ask his opinion about all of this to-do. But did it matter? She knew what he would tell her. She would be jobbernowl to seek out Charlie Gerber at the farm where she had been sending the escaped transportees two years ago.

Yet, if she did not, what was to prevent Mrs. Gerber from telling the authorities all she knew? Phoebe shivered. She should have guessed that those who might need Lady Midnight's help would share whispered confidences. No wonder, Jasper had sent this lady to her. He knew that not helping Mrs. Gerber could be more dangerous than helping her.

Not that it mattered. There was no other choice.

Seventeen

"Mrs. Gerber lives at the address you gave, my lady," Tate said, wearing the baffled expression as he rocked from one foot to the other. "She has two children, and her husband was sentenced to be transported for poaching. He has been gone for two years."

Phoebe did not release the curse banging against her lips. It would do her no good to own that she had hoped that Mrs. Gerber had been lying. That might have been far worse, because it would have suggested Mrs. Gerber had been sent here to trap her.

From where she sat by the window, she asked, "Has Mrs. Gerber been away from Bath recently?"

"Yes. There is talk that she went to London on some sort of business." He scratched his head. "I wasn't sure what to believe on that. What reason would a poor woman like her have in London?"

Instead of answering Tate's question, Phoebe asked, "And is there an old woman in the house?"

He nodded. "There is one, but she is very ill. One neighbor even told me she might already be dead, but the rest told me she was still barely alive."

"So it is true." She clasped and unclasped her hands. How much simpler it would have been if Mrs.

Gerber had been spinning a story for her in an attempt to trip her into confessing.

She should ignore the plea. Others would have tragedies and joys they could not share because they were hidden far from their families. Yet, she had never stood face-to-face with one of those who missed someone dear. The poor convicts who had been rescued from the ships were only shadows along the wharves or in the cellars on Grosvenor Square until they disappeared into darkened wagons.

But those in the shadows had discovered *her* identity. She ignored the hysterical laughter teasing the back of her throat. If she did nothing, she might endanger not only her households at Grosvenor Square and Brackenton Park, but Galen's as well. No one would believe that Galen was sucked into her crime only when he had saved her from the men chasing her. The tale he had told them when he had hidden her face against his shoulder in his carriage would now label him as guilty as she was.

She truly had no choice but to help Mrs. Gerber. Then, once Charlie Gerber had seen his dying mother and returned to where he was serving out the time of his sentence, she would find a way to make certain this did not happen again.

I want you to stop. The memory of Galen's voice resonated through her head along with the rest of the conversation. So assuredly she had told him that she could not halt this work that she had begun with such gullibility five years before. So coolly she had told him that she had no choice but to continue. Now those words were coming back to haunt her.

You have a choice. You could stop any time you wished. It had been simple for Galen to say that. She had tried to make him understand that she had made a pledge to save as many of these people as she could.

And you have.

With Galen's words raging through her memory, Phoebe came to her feet. "Tate, bring the carriage."

"Where are we bound, my lady?"

"Exmoor."

"Phoebe?" Galen stripped off his mud-splattered coat and tossed it onto a chair by the door. Striding into the parlor, he called Phoebe's name again.

"Do you have to shout?" Carr held one hand to his head. "Without Tate in the box, I have been bounced against the roof of the carriage too many times for a man with megrims."

"Your head would not be aching if you had not gotten yourself so in your cups that you got into another rough-and-tumble with those lads who were waiting to ambush you by that country tavern." Pushing his wet hair back out of his eyes, Galen turned to face his brother who had collapsed into a chair. Both of Carr's cheeks bore imprints left by knuckles. "If you would heed good sense just once, you might not find yourself in predicaments like that. I shan't always be about to untangle you from your messes."

Carr raised his eyes, revealing that one was already turning purple. "Because you are too busy playing court on Phoebe Brackenton?"

"You must own that it is a more pleasurable pastime than trying to avoid flying fists as I extract you from yet another fight." He went to the door to the garden. Although it was past dark and the rain had turned to a thick mist, he knew that Phoebe might have sought the quiet of the garden while she waited for him and Carr to return.

"So that is how it is going to be?"

Galen looked back at his brother who was now

struggling to his feet. "Carr, you are in no state to be discussing anything. Why don't you go to bed?"

"So you can find Phoebe and do the same?"

His fist struck Carr's chin before Galen had time to form a thought. As Carr reeled back, clutching his chin and bumping into a chair, Galen shook his hand. Years ago, he had learned that Carr's chin was hard.

Carr snarled a curse. Galen grasped his brother by the torn lapels as Carr added a crude insult about Phoebe.

Pushing his brother away, Galen said, "I have heard enough of this. I will accept your apology after I have spoken with Phoebe." He strode toward the door where Mrs. Boyd and Vogel were watching with identical horror on their faces.

"Why should I apologize for the truth?" shouted Carr. "Phoebe Brackenton may have a lady's title, but she is no better than the dockside whores she cavorts with."

"You don't know what you are talking about."

"I know she met you just outside the Little Lost Lamb. You know it is true, although both of you have denied it."

Galen took a deep breath. This lie had deteriorated before his brother's childish persistence in discrediting Phoebe. "Yes, it is true. But you are mistaken in your assumption. She was the lost lamb I offered to save from the wolves." Without pausing, he asked, "Mrs. Boyd, has Phoebe retired?"

"No." The housekeeper wrung her apron and glanced at Carr.

"Then please let her know I wish to speak to her as soon as I have washed up." Galen picked up his coat and folded it over his arm. He scowled at his brother before walking away along the hall.

Vogel hurried after him. "My lord," he said in a near whisper, "she is not here."

"Not here? Where is she?" He searched his mind but could not recall any invitations they had had for this evening.

Roland rushed toward him as Mrs. Boyd hurried up from the other direction. Again the expressions on his valet and the housekeeper matched the alarm on the butler's face.

"What is it?" Galen asked.

Mrs. Boyd motioned for them to follow. "This way, please."

Galen went into the antechamber of Phoebe's room. When he saw a bag sitting in the middle of the table, he growled an oath under his breath. He ripped it open and saw a change of clothes and a few personal items inside it. He started to ask a question, then paused when he saw the brocade box that held the ruby necklace set next to the bag.

He opened the box and lifted out a small slip of paper. Unfolding it, he read:

Dear Galen,

I have always considered myself a woman of courage, but my courage fails me now when I must take my leave. I thank you for all you have done. I wish I could stay longer. The obligations that are mine will not allow me to remain in Bath. If you do not wish to call upon me in London, I will understand. I hope you will come to understand that my heart chooses to stay with you even though I cannot.

Always yours,
Phoebe Brackenton

Putting it beneath his coat so it could not be read

by anyone else, although he suspected the housekeeper already knew its contents, Galen turned to Mrs. Boyd who stood in the open doorway and was now dabbing at her eyes with the corner of her apron. "You said she had left."

"Yes, my lord."

"Without her bag? Why would she return to London without her bag?"

Vogel glanced at the others, then said, "She did not go to London, my lord, although that may have been her intention."

"Then where is she?"

When the butler quickly explained how a woman had called and her desperate plea to Phoebe to help, horror descended on Galen.

"How could Phoebe be so foolish?" he asked.

"Foolish?" Mrs. Boyd's eyes snapped with sudden fervor. "Can't you see that she went to do whatever she must do in order to protect you? I heard her say to Tate as they were leaving that no one must know where they went."

Vogel nodded. "She told me as well that, under no circumstances, was I to receive this Mrs. Gerber again at Thistlewood Cottage. She said, 'This should not involve Lord Townsend. It is *my* problem.' " He scowled. "If I may say so, my lord, she has done whatever it is she has done to protect you."

"There would be no need for protecting anyone if she had not been so foolish." He slammed one fist against his other hand. "By Jove, she has gone beyond the bounds of common sense this time. How many more times does she think I can rescue her?"

Roland cleared his throat, then said, "Mayhap she has seen the many times you have come to Mr. Townsend's assistance and believes that you will do the same for her."

"No, Phoebe thinks I am witless for that." Galen swore under his breath when their faces revealed that they agreed with Phoebe. "I will not play nursemaid for Carr any longer. Nor will I let her put her very life in danger with her misplaced heroics."

"My lord?" asked Mrs. Boyd, confusion and dismay widening her eyes. "Lady Phoebe is in such a dire situation?"

"Not if I can get her out of it before she does something utterly want-witted. Where did they go?" Galen asked.

Quickly the butler repeated the directions he had heard Phoebe give to the coachman.

Galen smiled grimly. Phoebe's journey led to the near edge of Exmoor. It would not take him long to get there. Pulling on his filthy coat, he rushed out of the room and through the twisting corridors to the front door.

He shouted for the carriage to be brought.

A stableboy ran up. "My lord, Mr. Townsend just took the carriage. He said to tell you he would get more sympathy elsewhere."

"Then bring me a sturdy horse."

"Aye, my lord."

As the boy raced back to the stables, Galen sighed. Let Sandra Raymond offer Carr comfort. For the gold Carr gave her, she would commiserate with him and keep Carr away while Galen did what he must. He looked to the west. Phoebe had several hours' head start, but he must catch up with her before someone else did. And he had to ensure that she never had a chance to do something like this again. He was not certain how, but he would take whatever steps he must.

In the first light of dawn, the house resembled all

the others the carriage had passed on the moors. Isolated, it clung low to the hills that rolled up out of the sea. A few trees huddled around it as if the small house could protect them from the ravages of the wind that claimed these hills. Beyond it, sheep were puffs of earthbound clouds along the hillsides, vanishing into the fog that was creeping up from the water.

When Tate stopped the carriage, he jumped down and came around to open the door. Phoebe stepped out, avoiding the puddles that were left from the night's rain. She shivered, although the day was not cold. Every breath she took warned her how foolish she was being, but every heartbeat reminded her of what she would risk to have another chance to win Galen's heart. Only now did she understand that sometimes the choices were not clear.

A light breeze ruffled the grass around the buildings. The air was redolent with animal scents, and a wave of homesickness startled her. She had not guessed how much she had missed Brackenton Park.

"Are you certain this is the correct farm?" she asked, plucking at a loose thread on her gloves. She swallowed a yawn as she wished she had been able to sleep in the carriage during the trip from Bath.

Tate's face was long with distress. "I believe so, my lady."

"We shan't be long." She patted his arm.

"We should not be here at all."

Phoebe stared at him. "What do you mean?"

With the toe of his boot, he drew a circle in the dirt. "Lord Town—" He glanced about guiltily. "My lord has not been able to hide his concern about your safety. I do not know why he is anxious, but I trust that the reason has something to do with why you are here."

"Ask nothing more." Lying would gain her nothing

at this point. "Why don't you take the carriage back
to that tavern we passed where we turned off the main
road to come up to this farm?"

"And leave you here?"

"I will meet you there. It is not more than a mile
or two to the inn."

Tate glanced skyward. She guessed he was disappointed that he could not see a storm that would give
him the perfect excuse not to agree. "As you wish,
my lady. How long should I wait?"

"I will meet you there within two hours."

"As you wish, my lady," he repeated.

The carriage rolled back out onto the road that had
come to an end in this barnyard, and Phoebe turned
toward the house. She was not surprised when the
door opened as soon as the carriage vanished around
a corner. A brawny man with sun-bleached hair
walked toward her.

"Who are you?" he asked.

"I am here to speak with Charlie Gerber."

He rubbed his hand against the side of his nose,
then, yawning, pointed toward a paddock. "He usually
works over there."

Phoebe thanked the man and walked toward the un-
painted fence edging the field. By all that was blue,
she needed to have Jasper warn the farmers who took
in the escapees to take more care. The man should
not have given her this information without asking her
to provide some sort of proof that she knew Charlie
Gerber and had a good reason to speak with him.

One man was working in the paddock among a herd
of sheep. He was cutting out one sheep to shear it,
humming a quiet tune as he worked. He had a healthy
appearance about him. His dark hair fell forward into
his face, and his clothes were stained with dirt and
sweat.

"Are you Charlie Gerber?" she asked as he glanced toward her.

"Yes." He wiped his hands and squinted toward her. "Who are you?"

"A friend."

Putting his hands on the top rail, he stared at her. Then his eyes grew wide. "My lady!" He threw the gate open and rushed out, closing it behind him, so the sheep did not follow. "What are you doing here?"

"Is there somewhere we can speak without being overheard?"

"In the byre." His brown eyes were wide as he motioned for her to precede him into what was not much more than a lean-to built against the steep side of the hill.

Stronger animal odors struck her when she stepped into it. She was pleased to discover she could stand without hunching inside the building.

"What are you doing *here?*" Charlie asked.

"Your wife asked me to contact you to let you know that your mother is ill."

His face blanched. "Very ill?"

"I would not be here otherwise. There is a carriage waiting for us not far from here. We can get you to Bath and back for a quick call."

"But why are you here when—?"

"We do not have time to discuss this now."

"You are right about that, Lady Phoebe," said a voice from behind her.

Her arm was seized, and she was spun around. She gasped as she stared into a face she had hoped she would never see again. The last time she had seen him, his face had been shadowed as it was now. The last time she had seen him, he had been wearing a savage scowl as he was now. The last time she had seen him, he had been in the company of that odious sailor who had shot Jasper and she had been in Galen's arms as he had saved her from discovery.

"My lady," growled the man, "it seems that at last we meet face-to-face."

She heard Charlie groan, but she fought to keep her fear from showing. It would betray her. Meeting his eyes evenly, she said, "You have the better of me, sir. You know who I am, but I do not recall us being introduced."

"I am Captain Currie, master of the *Trellis*."

"You are far from the sea lanes here in Exmoor, Captain." She hoped her trembling was only within her.

When he smiled, she knew her hopes had been silly. "As you were far from where you should have been when you paid to have convicts removed from my ship, my lady."

"I believe you have mistaken me for another." She must keep up this pretense as long as she could. With a giggle, she asked, "Are you mistaking *me* for this Lady Midnight I have heard so much about?"

" 'Tis no mistake, my lady."

She giggled again as if she found all of this a charade put on for her entertainment. "Are you so sure of that assumption, Captain Currie? I was speaking with Captain Hill recently . . . a very disagreeable man." She widened her eyes. "A friend of yours, perchance?"

Captain Currie's mouth grew straight, and she knew he had taken insult just as she had hoped. "I do not do business with slavers."

"Nor do I, but Captain Hill was at a gathering I was attending last night, and you know how impossible it is to escape the boors who are determined to prey on their betters." She paused, again wanting to suggest she found him a match for Captain Hill's lack of manners. "He was speaking to me of this Lady Midnight, and I do believe he mentioned that her latest escapade took place while I was in Bath." Wrapping her arms around herself, she gave a shiver. "I was so glad I was not in London. Who knows what a woman like that might do? I daresay I shall stay in Bath until the whole matter is settled."

"That will be impossible. You must return to London."

"Why?" Again she widened her eyes in what she hoped would appear to be innocent shock. "I plan to attend more of the gatherings in Bath. They are so much more delightful than the ones in Town. Less crowded, and there is not so much emphasis on one making a match. I am in no hurry to go back to London."

Captain Currie looked past her. "Why are you here?"

"I missed the slower life of the country."

"So you came here instead of returning to Brackenton Park?"

"You ask many questions, Captain." Walking out of the byre as if she had no reason to be upset, she said, "Brackenton Park is several days' drive from Bath. Exmoor is not far, so I thought to come here to indulge in the opportunity to have a day in daisyville."

"A wasted tale, my lady," another man replied.

Phoebe whirled to look behind her. A trio of men stood between her and the road. Two were strangers, but the third was the man she had glimpsed when he had spoken to Jasper on the dock. This time, he held a gun openly.

"Who is this?" asked Captain Currie as he herded Charlie Gerber out of the byre.

"Someone who offered me no assistance in finding the house I have been looking for."

"Not a convict you smuggled off my ship?"

"You are being absurd. This man has been working here for—" She put her finger to her chin as she looked at Charlie. She yearned to shout that he must not panic. This situation was as dangerous as the night she had paid for his escape from *The Southern Cross*. "How long did you say?"

"Two lambing seasons, my lady."

Captain Currie pushed forward and grasped her arm again. "This silliness has gone on long enough. Come with me, my lady."

Phoebe considered resisting, but the fury in his eyes warned that he would drag her if she did. When she walked with him toward a waiting carriage, she glanced back at Mr. Gerber. He was staring at the ground. She wished she could offer him consolation that his chance to return to Bath had come to naught.

Or had it?

Mayhap she could still persuade Captain Currie that he was mistaken. Beginning to prattle like Mrs. Lyttle, she accepted his hand up into the carriage. She continued the bibble-babble when she sat on the cushion. She began to discuss every person at the duchess's gathering and what each had worn and her opinions of it. Even when Captain Currie sat beside her and the carriage began down the road, she did not dare to cease her chatter.

"Are you nervous, my lady?" he asked, his tone taunting.

"No, why would you ask that?" She laughed. "Why would I be nervous now when I had to face Captain Hill last night?" She did not let him answer as she began to list all of Captain Hill's disgusting actions last night, embroidering the story as she went.

Phoebe leaned forward as they reached the wider road that would lead out of the moors and back toward

Bath. If Tate was waiting by the carriage, she might be able to signal him in some way.

"Looking for someone?" Captain Currie asked.

"Why do you ask?"

"I thought I would save you from a great disappointment if you are seeking an ally."

She folded her hands in her lap and faced him with an expression of puzzlement. "You baffle me, Captain. I know you believe me to be this Lady Midnight, but I will be glad to assure anyone else as I assure you that—"

He laughed. Slanting toward her, he said, "Let me assure *you* that you do not have any allies. Townsend betrayed you, my lady."

"No!" she cried, her façade falling away. "He would not do that!"

"Do what?" He laughed. "Give testimony that you are, indeed, Lady Midnight?"

She fought not to collapse in tears. "How could he do that when no one knows who this Lady Midnight is?"

"Deny it if you will, but your charade has been revealed by one who should know. You cannot ignore that truth anymore than you will be able to ignore the judge's sentence that even your title will not save you from."

Eighteen

It was a night perfect for subterfuge. The moon was lost behind clouds, and the wind-driven rain blurred the few lights along the docks. By the wharves, the ships strained and creaked, eager to be on their way along the Thames and out to sea. Distant church bells sounded the hour as the poor huddling in the city's hovels tried to sleep while the *ton* gossiped and frolicked with flirtations through yet another early spring night.

The only thing missing, Phoebe knew, was her freedom. That had come to an end hours ago when a judge had pronounced her sentence. The trial had been a mockery, rushed through so fast that she suspected someone's pockets were now heavier with gold. She had hoped someone would be there to offer her support. Galen had not come, although she was unsure if he had even known about the trial. The only observers had been two women who were waiting for their nephew's case to be judged after hers. One sneezed all the way through the trial, the other wept . . . loudly and incessantly.

The judge had ignored them, for he had been interested in only one thing. He had ordered, "Tell me who helped you in this, my lady, and we can be lenient with you." He folded his arms on his desk and leaned forward to affix Phoebe with his stare.

"I told you that no one helped me." She kept her chin raised so the tears would remain to burn in the back of her eyes. It was ludicrous to be thinking of protecting Galen when he must have, in his zeal to protect Carr from his latest idiocy, revealed the truth by mistake.

The judge frowned at her. "My lady, I am giving you a chance to save yourself before I must pronounce sentence from the bench."

The barrister selected for her, because she had been given no chance to call her own, whispered, "You should heed him well, my lady. Honesty now may be your only salvation."

"But I am being honest," she said.

"You *honestly* expect me to believe that you, a well-born lady, could have masterminded the whole of this by yourself?" asked the judge.

She started to retort that she was more than capable of knowing the greed of underpaid sailors and the desperation of those who did not deserve to be banished from England forever. Then she realized her protests might betray the very people who had helped her. "Yes, I do."

"You give me no choice, my lady, but to sentence you to fulfill the term of the last person you took from Captain Currie's ship." He looked through his spectacles to the page spread in front of him. "That is seven years in the penal colony of Botany Bay."

Her protests that she was due a trial before a jury had not been heeded. How many times had she heard complaints from those she had rescued that they were guilty of no crime whatsoever and that they had been charged wrongly? She had not heeded them too closely, believing they should simply be grateful that

they had been given a second chance in England. Now
she knew she should have listened with more sympathy.

Phoebe walked away from the railing before she
joined the others who were weeping. As she went down
the steep steps into the ship's hold, which stank so badly
she feared she would be ill, she realized she should
be grateful that no one had given her a chance to send
a message to anyone. Jasper would have tried to rescue
her. If this was, as she suspected, an attempt to trap
those who had assisted her, no one must try to sneak
any of the convicts off before the ship sailed.

The deck rocked beneath her like something alive.
She ran her fingers lightly along the wall and winced
when a splinter sliced into one. She almost tripped
over someone who was crouched on the floor crying.
Unable to see if it was a man or a woman in the dim
light, she edged around the person.

Phoebe sank down against the wall as she heard
someone being sick somewhere in the darkness.
Something damp seeped through her gown, but she
did not move. She must accustom herself to these base
conditions if . . . A sob threatened to burst from her
throat. Drawing up her knees, she watched the shadows
move past. How many people would be stuffed
into this hold for the long journey?

She rested her cheek on her knees. She hoped that
someone would eventually let her household know
where she was. Jasper would know to contact Galen.
Tears weighed on her eyes. Galen . . . She had never
imagined she would meet a man who would make her
think twice about this crusade she had embarked on.
Nor had she guessed she would leave her heart behind
when she was banished to distant Australia. It was
tempting to imagine him boarding another ship to
chase after her and live with her in Botany Bay until

her sentence was over. How could he when he considered Carr his duty? He needed to be here to watch over his brother. She could not ask Galen to give up his obligations so they could be together. Not when she had been planning to leave Thistlewood Cottage to continue her duties.

One of the shadows screamed and dropped to the deck. Others shouted, fear building into panic.

Phoebe jumped to her feet and ran to the woman's side. Kneeling, she put her hand on the woman's head. She feared the woman had brought aboard one of the fevers that might keep the prisoners from surviving long enough to reach exile. The woman's skin was cool. She had swooned.

Knowing it was useless to ask for *sal volatile* aboard this ship, Phoebe chafed the woman's wrists until the woman's eyes fluttered open.

"Take slow breaths," Phoebe whispered.

"Oh, Jimmy. M'Jimmy," the woman moaned. "I shall ne'er see ye again."

A man sat beside her and nodded to Phoebe. "Thank ye, miss. She's m'daughter. I shall tend to 'er."

"Both of you are going to Australia?"

He nodded. "We'll 'ave each other at least."

Phoebe saw the envy on the faces around them and knew that few others would have a relative traveling with them. The tears grew heavier in her eyes, but she would not let them fall as she thought of never seeing her friends and family again.

Her name was shouted, echoing oddly through the space that must be larger than she had guessed, and she heard prayers being whispered. If these people thought she was here to save them, she must disappoint them. She could not save herself.

When her name was bellowed again, she pushed herself to her feet. She picked a path among the people sitting in the hold. The back of her gown clung to her with whatever had been wet on the deck. In a few days, she doubted if she would even notice.

A sailor was standing at the base of the companionway. "Cap'n wants to see ye."

"I do not wish to see him."

He gripped her arm so tightly she groaned. "Cap'n said he wants to see ye. So see ye he shall."

"Very well." She pulled her arm away and climbed the steep companionway. When she stepped out onto the deck, she stared in disbelief. Lamps hung overhead from the masts, but she did not look at them. Instead she stared at the lights of London, which were receding beyond the stern. They were already underway. In the depths of her grief, she had not noticed any change in the rhythm of the ship to alert her that they had set sail.

She took a deep breath. The smoke from the chimneys of Town had never tasted so precious. The breath exploded out of her when a hand in the middle of her back shoved her forward along the rocking deck. Her arm was taken again. This time, when she tried to jerk away, the sailor refused to release her.

He eyed her up and down. "We never had a fine lady like ye on the ship. 'Tis a right shame that ye have to stow with the rest of those who are going beyond."

She recognized the term that meant being sent to Australia as a convict. "I have no other choice."

"Aye, ye do." He rubbed his hand against the back of his mouth. "There be other quarters on this ship."

"No, thank you."

"So ye think ye be too fancy for the likes of me?"

Tempted to say yes, she turned away. She did not want to get into a brangle with this sea-crab. She wanted to catch a last glimpse of London. Even if she had not mortgaged everything she owned in the attempt to save some of these people from the too harsh laws, she would not have been allowed to bring funds with her to buy her passage home. She might never see London and her home again.

Another sailor, a cap settled just above his eyes, stepped in front of the man holding her arm. "Cap'n's waitin'," the second sailor said in a high-pitched voice that seemed too small for a man. Many of the sailors were not much more than boys.

"Then be out of m'way."

"*I* will take 'er to 'im."

Phoebe thought the first sailor would protest, but he nodded and shoved her toward the second man. She kept her feet with difficulty. When the second sailor put his hand on her arm, he did not clasp it as tightly as the first man had. Nor did he stare at her as if she were a harlot walking on the docks. She almost thanked him, then bit back her words. Any sign of clemency toward her might get this man punished. The tears grew heavy again. She had tried to protect her allies, but she might never know if she had succeeded.

As she stepped through a door into a cabin that was brightly lit and furnished with pieces that would not have been out of place in a dignified drawing room in Mayfair, she watched Captain Currie come to his feet. He was smiling broadly as he slapped a short lash onto his palm as if he were anxious to beat the truth from her. She shivered. That might not be far from what he was really thinking. Glancing past her, he said nothing as the sailor stepped out and closed the door.

"This is your last chance to name your assistants," the captain said. "I delayed the *Trellis* once from going to sea in order to stop you and your allies. I give you this one last chance before we head for open water."

"Don't you think that if I had had assistants I would have named them before this?" She folded her arms in front of her. "By all that's blue, do you think I *want* to be sent away from England?"

"I think you are protecting those who helped you." He sat on a gold-tufted chair. His poor manners told her that he now considered her one of the convicts. "You know it is futile."

"Yes, I do."

"What?" He sat straighter.

"It is futile to ask me to give you answers to your questions when I have already answered them and you choose to disregard what I say."

"I am waiting to hear you say that Lord Townsend was part of your cabal."

"I cannot say that, for it is not the truth." She hid her amazement that he was asking about Galen. Why hadn't he accused Galen of that when she was betrayed? Something was not right here. A sickening despair clamped around her. Her trial had been absurd, not a legitimate trial at all. Had it been only a sham to set a trap for someone else? Galen? But that made no sense if Galen had betrayed her—by accident or apurpose—to the authorities.

"Mayhap it is and mayhap it is not. At this point, my lady, you have spun so many tales for us that I cannot know what is true and what is a lie."

Phoebe opened the door. "Then I believe there is no need to continue this conversation."

Setting himself on his feet, he strode to her. "You will leave only upon my command."

"Captain Currie," she said coolly, "this is a convict ship, not a slave ship. I will give you the respect due to you as captain of this ship. In return, I expect you to offer me the respect due to me as Lady Phoebe Brackenton."

"You are a convict."

"A titled one, captain. My title was not taken from me." She kept her chin high. "I bid you good night. It has been an intolerably long day."

Phoebe fought to breathe normally as Captain Currie glowered at her. He opened his mouth, but the shout came from on deck. She whirled to see several men fighting. She could not make out which ones they were because the lanterns hanging from the masts rocked with the motion of the ship.

"Take her below!" Captain Currie ordered, pushing her toward the second sailor who had brought her to his cabin.

"Aye, Cap'n," he replied in his squeaky voice as he took her arm. "This way, m'lady."

"What is happening?" she asked.

He chuckled, keeping his head lowered. "Don't worry yerself, m'lady. Some of the lads don't want to go to Australia any more than ye do. Cap'n will get their attention."

Phoebe swayed with the motion of the deck as the sailor led her closer to the railing so they could avoid the fisticuffs. Shouts seemed to come from every direction. A man ran past her, knocking her into the railing. She gasped and clutched onto the rail when a section of it swung open. That was where they had come aboard. Someone must not have latched it securely.

"C'mon," the sailor holding her arm ordered. "Time to get you away from this fight."

"Yes," she said as a man shrieked with pain.

"Good luck, Lady Phoebe," the sailor murmured, his accent abruptly gone as his voice deepened.

She stared at him as he drew off his cap. "What?

Jasper!" She could not believe what her eyes were showing her.

His answer was a shove. She rocked backward and reached to grasp the railing. She caught one side as her other arm windmilled. Jasper tore her fingers off the railing. He pushed her again.

This time, she fell. Did someone else scream or was that her? She had no time to guess before she struck the water. Fighting her way back to the surface, she looked in every direction. If the *Trellis* bore down upon her, she would be killed.

Her sigh of relief bubbled against the waves when she saw she had been propelled far away from the ship. Her relief became disbelief when two more splashes came from closer to the *Trellis*. Someone else was in the water. A shout of "Man overboard" rang out from the ship's deck. She started to swim toward the person, but a hand grasped the back of her soaked gown.

Looking over her shoulder, she saw Jasper. With a chuckle, he said, "This way, my lady. Fast as you can now."

"Can you swim?" she asked, spitting out water as the wake from the ship lapped her face. "Is your leg strong enough?"

"Follow me." He began a clumsy stroke that propelled him with surprising ease through the murky waters of the river.

Phoebe did. The skills she had learned as a child in the pond at Brackenton Park were rusty, but she managed to paddle toward the shore. Abruptly the shadows thickened in front of her. A small boat! If it was from the *Trellis* . . .

Her arm was grabbed. She started to scream, then choked on the sound as she looked up into Galen's face. Lines were deepened by the darkness. Grasping his arms, she let him help her scramble into the boat. Jasper crawled aboard and grabbed the oars, pushing them away from the *Trellis* and toward some trees that were overhanging the river.

Phoebe began, "How did you—?"

Putting his finger to her lips as he had so often, Galen drew her down into the wet puddle at the bottom of the small boat. He pulled a tarpaulin that stank of fish and stagnant water over them. In the dark cave beneath it, he put his arm around her.

She rested her cheek against his chest that was bare above his half-buttoned shirt. He must have been portraying a local fisherman because he wore denim pantaloons and scuffed boots. Running her finger along the skin revealed by his open shirt, she closed her eyes and savored the wondrous texture.

He tilted her face up as his mouth captured hers. The hunger in his kiss matched the need she had feared would never be fulfilled. When he pulled her closer, her wet clothes should have steamed with the heat that washed through her, threatening to overmaster her. His lips swept away the water on her neck as he lathered it with kisses.

"That was close," he whispered in her ear.

"What do you mean?"

"I nearly lost you to the far side of the world."

"Yes, you did." She drew up her knees as she had on the ship and leaned back against a slat that must be a seat. "Why did you come to save me? Were you trying to assuage part of your large load of guilt?"

"Guilt?" He opened a dark lantern, because the light would not seep through the tarpaulin. His eyes narrowed. "At what?"

"Captain Currie—"

"Who?"

"The master of the *Trellis*. The ship I was on. He

told me that you had betrayed me to the authorities." She took his sleeve that was as wet as she was. "He told me that you had led him to me."

"Me? Phoebe, I love you. I would never betray you."

Her fingers clenched on his sleeve. "You love me?"

He swept his fingers up through her wet hair and pulled her mouth to his. The slow, deep kiss left her quivering as he drew back enough to say, "I had thought that you would have guessed by now."

"You never said."

"And I never said that you were involved with the escaped convicts."

"Even when I told you that you were stupid to let your brother twist your life about?"

"Even when you told me that and made me realize what a beef-head I have been." He clasped her face between his hands. "Yes, I was furious with you, but I would never betray you. What gave you the idea that I would do that?"

"Captain Currie told me that you had let the authorities know where I was when I went to see Charlie Gerber."

He tapped her nose. "Going to see one of the vanished convicts was your first mistake, but believing that cur was your second."

"You did not come to my trial, so what was I to think?"

"I was busy." His lips brushed hers lightly. "Arranging to keep you from being sent so far away."

"But Captain Currie said . . ." Her eyes widened. "He said *Townsend*."

"Carr must have sent them after you." Galen drew back the tarpaulin and stared at the shore that was only a few boat lengths away.

"Yes."

"Because he is jealous."

"Of me?"

Galen nodded. "You were right that he was using me. My sense of duty to my family became his tool to manipulate me. He fears that if I turn my attention to you, then he will no longer be able to depend on my coming to his rescue." He laughed. "I don't want to come to anyone's rescue any longer. I want to live a quiet life with the woman I love."

Her smile faded. "But I have been convicted and sentenced to be sent to Australia for seven years."

"My family has a hunting lodge far to the north in Scotland. We will go there until we can have the mockery of your sentence overturned."

"Mockery? You know about it?"

He glanced at Jasper who sneezed and sneezed.

"You!" Phoebe cried. "Jasper, how could you be so daring?"

"Lord Townsend was busy arranging to hire this boat and horses to get us away from here." He pointed to the shore where a lad waited with three horses. "I sneezed, and Johnson wept." He laughed. "I never thought anyone would think *he* was an old woman."

She smiled, trying to reconcile her butler with the woman in the gallery. It was impossible.

"Captain Currie wants to implicate you as well, Galen. That was why he allowed me out of the hold."

"He overplayed his hand there." He chuckled. "My alibi is legitimate."

"Almost."

The boat gently struck the riverbank, and Galen handed her ashore. She looked at where the *Trellis* was vanishing into the night. So close she had come to losing everything. She gazed up at Galen. Some things—like this wondrous love—were just too precious to risk.

"I love you, too," she whispered, slipping her fingers through his.

"It is about time you said so."

"I thought you knew by this time, and by this . . ." She gave him a teasing kiss. "What happens if you cannot get my sentence overturned?"

"Then we shall be banished to Scotland for seven years until you can reenter the Polite World." He gave her a rakish grin. "I almost hope it isn't overturned. Then I shall have you all to myself for the next seven years."

"Only seven years?"

"Forever." He locked his hands behind her waist. "You shall be *my* Lady Midnight."

She drew his mouth toward hers. "Yes, and all my midnight adventures shall be with you."

Author's Note

His Lady Midnight is based—very loosely—on the eighteenth conspiracy of Member of Parliament Thomas Benson, who arranged to be paid to transport convicts to the American colonies. Instead of taking them to America, he left them at Lundy Island, north of the Devonshire coast. There, he brought tobacco from the American colonies and used the convicts to help him smuggle it into England.

My next Zebra Regency will be *A Guardian's Angel,* available in January 2002. A young woman, hired as a guardian for a lass who has lost her father, finds herself caught up in the middle of an argument that has torn two good friends apart. Can she heal so many hearts and still safeguard her own?

I like hearing from my readers. You can contact me by email at: jaferg@erols.com, or by mail at:

Jo Ann Ferguson, P.O. Box 575, Rehoboth, MA 02769. Check out my web site at:
www.joannferguson.com

Happy reading!

More Zebra Regency Romances

Embrace the Romances of
Shannon Drake